ANOTHER CHANCE
FOR LOVE

A LAKE CHELAN NOVEL, BOOK 8

SHIRLEY PENICK

Photography by Wander Aguiar

Cover Models: Wander Aguiar and Megan Napolitan

Contact me:

www.shirleypenick.com

www.facebook.com/ShirleyPenickAuthor

To sign up for Shirley's New Release Newsletter, sign up on my webpage or send email to shirleypenick@outlook.com, subject newsletter.

To all of us who have passed the first blush of youth: We are strong because we've fought through the battles of life. We are beautiful because we have finally accepted ourselves and have the confidence to back that up. We are compassionate and kind because we've seen that everyone goes through tough times and sometimes a person needs a helping hand. And just because we might have a few wrinkles or sagging skin, we know that we are never too old to fall in love.

CHAPTER ONE

*C*arol Anderson watched as the ferry pulled into the landing, the white boat a stark contrast to the deep blue lake, the brown mountains on the other shore, and the bright blue sky. It didn't matter that she'd seen this same view many times in her fifty-two years, she still loved it. She waved at the captains she'd known all of her life, and stood to the side as they pulled out the gangplank for people to walk off the ferry.

It was a passenger ferry only, so no cars to avoid, if a person wanted to bring their car to Chedwick they would have to use the barge. A car wasn't really necessary to visit their town. It was small enough to walk everywhere, and there were a few shuttles for people, to get to and from the amusement park, if they didn't want to walk.

Carol saw her guest and greeted the man as he came off the ferry with an outstretched hand and a smile on her face. "Wes, it's so good to see you again. Welcome back to Chedwick." As their hands touched, she felt a zing of attraction she hadn't felt in too many years to count. It shocked her right down to her toes, because she'd spent a fair amount of time with Wes Radcliff—the last time he was in town—to work on some architectural drawings for the wedding venue at Amber's restaurant, and nothing like this had occurred.

He cleared his throat and said, "I'm Max Radcliff, Wes's twin brother, he couldn't make it this time, so I came instead. We're both architects and work closely on projects. Sorry for the confusion. Are you Mayor Carol?"

She pulled her hand from his and tried to cover her reaction. "Oh, my, excuse my forwardness, Wes never mentioned a twin. I *am* Carol Anderson, but I haven't been the mayor for a half-dozen years."

His brown eyes sparkled with mirth and she wondered if he was laughing at her. Had he noticed her reaction to that simple touch? She felt like an idiot, or like a grade school child. For goodness sake, she had grandchildren in grade school. *Knock it off and act like the professional woman you are.*

Max said, "Not to worry, you wouldn't be the first person to get us mixed up."

Now that she knew better, she could see the differences between this man and his brother. His beard and his salt and pepper hair were both a little longer and a little wilder. There was a touch of sadness she sensed, that had not been apparent in Wes. The most obvious difference was the pulse of attraction she'd felt when their hands had touched. She was going to ignore that.

She'd been staring at him long enough. "I do see some faint differences. Well let's get going. Do you need help carrying anything? My car is just over there." She waved her hand toward the parking lot.

He smiled and picked up his bag and portfolio. "No help needed, lead on. Thanks for picking me up, Wes said it was a short walk to your Bed and Breakfast."

"It isn't far, but carrying luggage even that short a

distance isn't fun. Picking people up from the landing is one of the services I provide for my guests."

Once they were in the car with Max's luggage in the back, Carol said, "I'll give you a quick tour, so you know where everything important is. First the church, since that's where you'll be spending most of your time."

He chuckled. "Not my normal stomping grounds. But that is what the architectural plans in my portfolio are for, a larger chapel with offices and classrooms above part of that, so you're right. I will be spending most of my time there. At least during the day."

When they reached the church, he asked her to give him one minute to look at the foundation that was ready for building to commence. She was happy to let him wander the grounds while she watched. It was such a pretty summer day that she wasn't in any hurry to get back to her B&B.

He had a long-legged stride and an intensity that showed he really cared about his work. As she watched, she felt a fascination with his movements and couldn't help speculating about her response to their hands touching. What was that, some kind of lust? She really had no idea, she'd only ever had one man in her life, and they'd started out in grade school. She didn't need the complications of a man after so many years alone, so she pushed her thoughts to the side and just watched. He took some measurements with a laser tool, nodding as he went. When he was done, he walked back toward her car and climbed in.

"Looks good. I think we can begin building."

"Great. The old sanctuary is too small for some of the larger weddings people have asked about booking. The sooner we can get it done the better."

"That's why I'm here, to get it started and any questions answered. Or minor modifications drawn up."

"We do appreciate your dedication and time away from your family and friends."

Carol noticed that he'd tensed when she mentioned family and she wondered if there was something going on there. It didn't take him long before he relaxed again, but he didn't comment, so she let it go and drove him around town. She showed him the other places he would want to know about, the city offices, the little store, Greg's bar, and Amber's restaurant.

Max took note of all the places Carol was showing him. He had a tourist map he'd picked up and studied on the long ferry trip from Chelan. Many of the things she was pointing out were on the map but not all of them, so he wanted to remember where they were to mark them on his map. It was a tiny city, not much bigger than a couple of football stadiums, from what he could see, but it seemed to have all the amenities, that's all he really cared about.

He'd been surprised by Mayor Carol, no, former mayor now. His brother had never once mentioned what a beautiful woman she was. Her bright blue eyes had stopped him in his tracks. Of course, Wes was happily married, and had been forever, as had he, until that fateful night. It was nearly the sixth-year anniversary of his beloved wife's death, this month in fact. He still missed Jeanette with a strength that sometimes took his breath away.

Was that why Wes had sent him to Chedwick? Thinking it would keep him occupied and help avoid the funk that normally assailed him as the date of her death approached. It might work. He did love to supervise the start of a build, and he hadn't had much on his plate, so spending a couple of weeks in this little town might be good for him. Not that he would admit that to his brother.

And the other thing he had no intention of admitting, even to himself, was the immediate attraction he'd felt to Carol Anderson. When their skin had met, he'd felt... a disturbance in the force, was what had leapt to his mind. There'd been a jolt of electricity that had shot up his arm and then spread throughout his body. He thought she might have noticed it too, but he wasn't positive about that.

She was the direct opposite of his dark haired, tall and lanky wife. Carol Anderson was a head shorter than he was, so about five foot five, with shoulder-length blonde hair and the most compelling bright blue eyes. She was curvy in all the right places and looked to be fit. Her hand was strong and not completely soft. Calluses held testament to a woman who worked.

Despite her attractions, Max wasn't interested in starting something up. He would keep their interaction professional and ignore any other sparks.

He was glad she was showing him around town so he could get his bearings. It was going to be a novel experience, staying in this tiny town with no vehicle. Everything was within walking distance, but he'd need to take his portfolio and laptop to the job site, so it would be interesting, to say the least.

The Queen Anne Victorian house that held his temporary residence was lovely. The architecture was pleasing to the eye and the color scheme was perfect, nothing too ostentatious. Some people with Victorian houses painted them the most obscure colors. Carol had painted hers a dusky blue, with white accents, and dark blue shutters, and then used brightly colored flowers to make the place pop.

She parked her Subaru Outback behind the house in a

small parking lot, and popped the hatch open so he could retrieve his luggage. He followed her in the back door to where she could check him in, and give him the key to his room. He was pleasantly surprised to note the décor inside, was just as classy as the outside of the house. Jeanette would have loved it; her interior designer eye would have very likely chosen to outfit the rooms exactly as they were. He was going to feel very much at home, providing the bedrooms weren't too frilly.

Carol's voice pulled him away from his musings. "I thought you might enjoy the attic room, it's got better light and a private bath, rather than sharing with everyone else on one of the lower floors. It will be more stairs; you don't have any knee or hip problems, do you?"

"No, I don't. I'm sure it will be perfect."

Her eyes held a bit of sadness. "It's a great room and was mine until a year ago when I fell and had hip surgery. I couldn't manage all the stairs for a while and my kids convinced me to move to a lower floor."

"I'm sorry to hear that."

Carol shrugged. "Life happens. The room I'm in now is nice and it was the master, so it has a private bathroom too, but it's also got memories. I moved to the attic room not long after my husband passed. Leaving the master bedroom unused always bothered me, and then when the kids moved out, and all the rooms were unused, it nagged at me. I tried to determine what to do about it. I didn't want to sell, so that's when I decided on a B&B."

Max knew all about fighting memories. He'd sold the home he'd had with Jeanette after three years, hoping it would help him to move on. It had helped… some, not enough, but some. "I totally understand. I did sell my home a few years after my wife's death."

Carol sighed. "Life is hard sometimes. But we just keep on truckin', don't we?"

6

She flashed him a pretty smile and he felt a comradery he'd missed. Rather than think about that too much, he said, "We do. I'll go get settled in."

He'd made it up all those stairs and was happy to note that he wasn't winded, so it would be no burden at all to be in the attic. The room was great. It did have wonderful natural light, a large private bathroom that Carol must have had put in, and it wasn't the least bit frilly. There was a gorgeous quilt on the bed that he doubted he would need while he was in town for the summer, but the colors in it made the room cheery.

The desk would easily accommodate his laptop and there were two comfy looking chairs in front of what looked like a gas fireplace. Max doubted the original attic would have had a fireplace, so it was a nice touch. He could almost see Carol puttering around in this room, sitting in one of the chairs in front of the fireplace, maybe reading a book and sipping hot chocolate. Laughing at himself he opened his suitcase, he didn't even know if Carol liked hot cocoa or reading. However, he was certain he would be very comfortable in this room for the week or two he was in town.

CHAPTER TWO

*C*arol bustled about getting breakfast ready. The place was packed and probably would continue to be, right on through August, maybe even part of September. Although when school started it wouldn't be families going to the amusement park. No, then it would be art lovers and older couples out to enjoy the fall weather before the cold hit. Maybe a wedding party or two, although the majority of those were in May and June.

She loved running her B&B. After she'd fallen, she'd brought on a little more help to handle the running up and down on the stairs and some of the heavier tasks. When her daughter, Sandy, had spent the summer helping while she recovered and got her strength back, she had given her some good suggestions. Ideas to help things run smoother. Carol supposed that was the engineer and project manager in her asserting itself. But they'd been good suggestions and although Carol didn't want to admit it, her recovery had taken longer than she'd thought it would.

Everything was fine now, and she would keep the extra help. The inn was in the black and could afford it, so why run herself ragged when she didn't need to? She still kept plenty busy, but she didn't have to devote twenty-four hours a day, and that was just fine with her. Having lunch out with friends or fussing with her flowers outside was a nice change of pace.

She pulled the frittata out of the oven. It was the last thing that needed to be set out. The cinnamon rolls were iced and on the buffet table, Judy had cut up the fruit and made the fresh-squeezed orange juice. There was a large urn of coffee and a few other juices as well as milk for the kids. Bacon and sausage were piled high. Even though the frittata had ham in it, she knew people would eat the breakfast meats. There were also bagels and several types of breads for toast, if people preferred, along with a selection of cereals.

She placed the frittata in the warming pan and shut the lid just as Max walked in, looking all freshly scrubbed and ready for the day. She wondered if he smelled as good as he looked. The man filled out his jeans pretty damn well for a man his age. He put his portfolio and backpack at a small table and walked over to the buffet.

"Good morning, Max. I hope you slept well, was the room satisfactory?"

He'd made a beeline for the coffee and was filling a cup. "The room is perfect, and I can see why you chose it as your own. I slept just fine and am ready to face the day."

His gaze swept over the buffet. "It looks like there is enough food here to feed an army, and so many choices. Is that a frittata I smell?"

Carol lifted the lid she'd just shut. "It is indeed. I just brought it out so it's piping hot."

"Excellent." He lifted the lid on the home-made rolls and groaned. "You're trying to kill me; those cinnamon buns look delicious. Did you make them from scratch?"

His groan skittered through her and took her on a path

that had nothing to do with food. She mentally shook herself and forced her mind to concentrate. "I did."

"So, you got up at what three o'clock in the morning so they could rise and everything?"

"Not at all, I got up much later than that… I got up at three-thirty."

Max chuckled as she'd intended him to. She grinned at him for appreciating her joke.

Their eyes locked for a second and then he cleared his throat and looked away. "Well I better have one of those, since you worked so hard on them. And some of that frittata, too. I'll just bet that's fresh-squeezed orange juice, isn't it?"

She picked up her kitchen mitts. "Of course! Enjoy your breakfast and good luck on the church building."

She left Max filling his plate and hurried back into the kitchen, where she had exactly nothing to do. What had that look been about? It had felt strange and compelling and scary all at the same time. She didn't like it one little bit, except she kind of did like it. It was exciting, scary, but exciting.

Max put some of the yummy egg dish on his plate. It looked like it had ham and potatoes and spinach in it, with lots of cheese. The cinnamon buns were dripping with frosting and huge. He also found some nice crispy bacon and took several pieces of that, and a glass of the fresh squeezed orange juice.

Good grief, he never ate this much for breakfast. He whipped up a couple of eggs twice a week and the rest of the time it was cereal, mostly cold cereal. In the winter he might make some hot cereal as long as all he had to do was add hot water and stir.

But he could appreciate a fine breakfast as much as the next guy. It was probably good he would be walking everywhere, to burn off the calories he was going to be eating, with Carol making such delicious food.

As he ate the exquisite breakfast, he pondered the look he'd shared with Carol. They seemed to have some sort of affinity for each other. Maybe it was just the similar age and experience they had, yeah that was it. They'd both lost their spouses, they were both in their fifties, that was all it was, just similar circumstances.

Yep, that was it. And wasn't he getting good at lying to himself.

But he was here to do a job, so he slapped the lid shut on the thoughts and feelings trying to make themselves known and finished his breakfast. There was a family of five that had come in and he enjoyed watching the antics of the children. Another couple sat in a corner, more interested in each other, than in their food.

He needed to get moving. The construction meeting would begin in a half hour and would keep him occupied the rest of the day. Max noticed a tray for dirty dishes and placed his on there. Then he filled his thermos with coffee and headed out for the day. He would have said goodbye to Carol, but she was nowhere to be found. Besides that, she was the hotel owner, not his best friend.

Shaking his head at his foolishness, he walked outside into the summer day. It was still cool this morning, but he didn't doubt for one minute that it would end up being a scorcher.

CHAPTER THREE

$\mathcal{M}$ ax couldn't have been happier with the building project. They were three days into it and it was progressing at a surprising rate. The meeting on the first day had included all the key players, and their professionalism and enthusiasm battled in his mind for supremacy.

They had a strong desire to have the new sanctuary finished by Christmas. That desire was fueling the work. It was a very rapid plan, since the outer structure would need to be up and weather-proof in about eight weeks. If Max had heard that idea, before he'd met the people involved, he would have laughed and replied with a 'no way in hell' kind of comment. But once he'd met with the group and they had talked through their plans, he had gotten on board with their desire and had helped to discuss what could be put off until after Christmas.

He still wasn't sure they could pull it off, but it wouldn't be on his account. He'd decided to extend his stay in Chedwick by a week, to be of help. Their enthusiasm was contagious.

What Max wasn't so sure of, was Carol Anderson. He'd seen her every morning during breakfast, and just the thought of the truly scrumptious food she served made his mouth water.

But the woman herself was so skittish. She would be out in the eating area chatting with one of the other residents, and when he walked in, she nearly ran out of the room, with some excuse to replenish the food, and then he didn't see her again the rest of the morning.

Max couldn't figure it out. Sure, there had been some attraction on his part, but he wasn't a monster, he didn't bite. He showered, so he didn't stink. He hadn't made a pass or acted an ass, so he really had no idea why she seemed to be avoiding him. It didn't matter since he wasn't here for her, but he wished he could calm her fears.

With a shrug for his thoughts, he stepped into the Pizza place, the rich aroma of marinara, garlic, and oregano assailed his nostrils and he grinned. He was going to get an enormous pie, fully loaded. Some of it might end up going back with him to eat for a few days, but that was just fine with him. Cold pizza, or even reheated pizza, was one of God's greatest gifts. And a cold brew to go with it would sit well. They only had bottled beer, but that was just fine with him.

The hostess, a woman with frizzy gray hair and a nametag that read Sylvia, said, "We're a little crowded tonight, with a baseball team's after game, win celebration. Do you want to wait, or would you mind being seated at a table with another resident of the town?"

Max had nothing against sitting with someone from the town. It would be fun to get to know someone not associated with the build. "Seated with someone would be fine, as long as they don't mind."

"Not at all, we asked ahead of time, knowing it would be a busy night."

"Then by all means, lead the way."

He followed the hostess into a large room where there was indeed a baseball team and a lot of parents taking up the entire middle of the room. There were only a few tables around the edges that were filled with other people.

Sylvia dodged and weaved past the crowd of highly excited baseball players and headed toward the far corner of the room. He couldn't see past the melee or Sylvia, so he just followed her through the noise and commotion.

She eventually stepped to the side and gestured to the only chair left in the restaurant, directly across from Carol Anderson. Damn, now what was going to happen?

Carol looked up when Sylvia said, "Here is your dinner companion for the evening Mayor... um I mean Carol, shit, still not used to that. I'm guessing this fine architect is staying in your B&B so it's not even a stranger. Thanks for sharing your table."

Carol muttered something like "You're welcome" under her breath as her eyes met his and then darted around the room, like a frightened bird.

He'd had enough of that nonsense, so he sat down and took the menu from Sylvia.

Sylvia said, "A waitress will be right over to take your order. Enjoy."

When Sylvia had marched off, he said, "I don't bite. I'm going to have a brew and an enormous amount of pizza. So, you've got nothing to fear."

Carol looked a little sheepish. "I'm not afraid."

"Riiiight."

"No really, I don't think you're going to bite. It's just... well, if you must know, I... dammit, I am not a teenager, I'm a grown professional woman, who has been acting like an idiot. All because I find you attractive."

That startled him. He'd felt magnetism, too, but when she'd avoided him for three days, he'd figured it was one-sided and he needed to ignore it.

"There I said it and now it's over. I'm not the least bit interested in starting anything. I've been a widow for over twenty-five years and I'm perfectly happy in that place."

All right, not exactly what he was expecting, or maybe it was *exactly* what he was expecting. "Carol, you are a very beautiful woman and while I would be happy to engage in a romp, or two, in the sheets with you, I'm not looking for anything either. I'm not sure I can love again. I've already had the love of my life; my heart was buried with her."

Carol felt like the lowest form of life. Here the man was still grieving his wife, and she'd been acting like an idiot. She'd avoided him like the plague, acting like some teenager with a crush, instead of like the hostess of her Bed and Breakfast.

She felt her face flame in embarrassment, but she was by-God going to act like a grownup. "I'm sorry for my actions, Max. I just have never felt that kind of attraction before and I didn't know what to do with it. My husband and I loved each other deeply, but it was built over a lifetime. So, when I felt the powerful electricity between us, I guess I reverted to my teenage self, all awkward and hiding from the cutest guy in school."

The waitress interrupted their conversation and she barely heard Max order an extra-large pizza with all the toppings and a beer. While he was busy, she took a large sip of wine for some liquid courage.

When the waitress moved off, he said quietly, "So, can we

move on now, and be friends? I have a few questions I would like to ask the former mayor of the town."

Carol blessed him for not making a fuss and was more than happy to answer questions. "Yes, of course. Ask away."

"Great, but one last personal issue. Any interest in a romp in the sheets?" He waggled his eyebrows to indicate he was teasing her.

Her face flamed again. "No. I don't think so. I've only ever been with one man and the last time was over twenty-five years ago. I'm not sure I know how it all works anymore."

Max's eyes sparkled and he waggled his eyebrows. "It's like riding a bike. Or, I would be more than happy to remind you."

She laughed at his teasing. "No, thanks. I'll pass."

"Let me know if you change your mind. Now back to those questions."

Carol was happy to move on to his inquiries. They spent a pleasant evening talking about town workings and eating delicious pizza.

CHAPTER FOUR

*N*ow that she'd gotten the silliness of her attraction to Max taken care of, Carol could go about her normal day without feeling like she had to hide from him. It had been a foolish reaction in the first place, but the last time she'd felt anything like that had been in high school, which was too many years ago to count. So, she gave herself a pass on acting like a fool. An old fool.

They had walked back to the B&B in easy companionship, she'd offered to move things around in the fridge so he could put his leftover pizza in it.

Max shook his head. "No need for that. I'll just take it to my room. I like it at room temp."

"But it should be refrigerated."

"Not to worry, I've been leaving leftover pizza on the counter for years and it hasn't killed me yet."

Carol had shuddered at the idea, but he was a grown man and she was not his mother. She'd put her leftovers in the fridge. She actually had two refrigerators, one she used for the B&B and one that was personal. She didn't mind if guests left their leftovers in her personal one. That left the B&B fridge safe from odd smells, she primarily used it for breakfast foods, so using it for that strict purpose ensured the breakfasts were purer.

She'd decided on making coffee cakes this morning. Carol always had a menu plan, but sometimes when she was feeling creative, she veered from it. Today was one of those days. The counter was filled with all the baking ingredients she'd used. The aroma of cinnamon filled the air as the fancy twisted pastries baked. When they were finished, she would bake the blueberry ones that were waiting their turn in the oven. She might cut off a small piece of one of the cinnamon ones, while it was still warm and slather it in butter.

Bustling about, she put away all the baking ingredients and scrubbed down the counters, before pulling out the breakfast meat. Today she was serving link sausages and fried ham slices. Just plain old, scrambled eggs would do since she'd spent longer on the pastries than normal. Her enormous cast-iron skillet would cook all the sausage in one pan, she just had to keep rotating them, both on their axis and also around in the pan.

Music was on low, so she didn't wake anyone, but she rocked around the kitchen as she cooked. She'd been raised on rock and roll, and she still loved it to this day. When she knew the house was empty, she turned the volume up to eardrum shattering levels and danced like a crazy woman. If she didn't live in the boonies, she would probably be one of those crazy people that attended every concert within five hundred miles. But she did live in the boonies and she had a B&B to run, which didn't lend itself to traveling for concerts.

She was rocking out to Aerosmith, using a wooden spatula as a microphone, when she sensed she wasn't alone anymore. She froze and turned toward the door to find Max leaning against the door jam, with an amused expression on his face.

Her face flamed, but then she chose to own it. "If you don't dance when Aerosmith is rocking the house, then you must be an alien or maybe a droid."

He chuckled. "True enough, unless I'm happily watching a pretty woman rock it enough for both of us."

"Points for the comeback and the flattery."

"Comeback, yes. Flattery, no. Just the facts, ma'am."

She giggled at the Dragnet reference, and thought she would ignore the rest. She had to admit that, for just one second, she felt a little thrill at a good-looking man calling her pretty. It had been a few years. She knew she was attractive, she had a mirror, but she'd been an authority figure in town for so many years that no one would think to call her pretty. Not that she needed it, but it was nice to hear. "So, did you need something?"

"Just thought I would come see if there was coffee on. I woke up early and opted to get some design work done. It's not urgent, so I work on it whenever I get the time. But any kind of work before coffee is futile."

"Yes, I did start the coffee, even though it's a little early for breakfast. It's never too early for java."

"Agreed. If you don't mind, I'll fill up my thermos and take it back to my room. Are you burning those sausages?"

Carol whirled around and quickly turned the sausages, some were a little darker than she liked but there were a lot of people in the world who liked them nearly burnt. She would pile the worst of them at the back of the warmer and let people select them if they wanted.

Max returned with his coffee. "I'll get out of your hair, so you don't burn the rest of the breakfast. I don't want a mob after me for distracting the cook."

She laughed as he headed back up the stairs. The timer for the coffee cake dinged, so she pulled out the cinnamon ones and popped in the blueberry.

Max trudged back up the stairs to his room in the attic. He'd been shocked to find Carol dancing up a storm in her kitchen while she cooked sausages and baked something that smelled delicious in the oven.

He'd been enjoying the show with a little bemusement and a whole lot of lust. The woman was built and could really shake it. He could have stood and watched her all day, but she'd either seen him reflected in some appliance or had sensed him, because she froze like a deer in headlights and had turned slowly toward him. He didn't know if the color in her cheeks was embarrassment or from the wild dancing in the warm kitchen. Maybe both.

Max knew they had no business getting involved and he wasn't going to go there, but if things were different, he would. Yes, he would. The woman mesmerized him, and she didn't have to be doing a damn thing. He was pretty sure she could be asleep, and he would feel the same, but with her color high and her eyes sparkling from dancing to an old rock and roll song, which just happened to be a favorite of his, wow, just wow.

When he got to his room, rather than heading back to his computer and the CAD drawing he was working on, he pulled out his sketchbook and some charcoal. A few quick lines and Carol came to life on the page, some shading and details and he had a very nice remembrance of the event.

He fussed with it a few more minutes until his phone chimed with the wakeup alarm. Max shook his head at himself, he'd managed to waste the extra time he'd had, on a delightful sketch of Carol Anderson. He would frame it when he got home. A souvenir of his time in the town and a reminder that he still felt desire for a woman.

He would always love his wife and miss her, but it was good to know his sexuality hadn't been buried with her.

CHAPTER FIVE

When the doorbell rang, Carol nearly dropped the pitcher of lemonade she was returning to the fridge. She'd had her book club last night and it was left over. She couldn't figure out why someone would ring the doorbell, this was a business, but it shouldn't have startled her enough to drop the pitcher. As she quickly walked to the front of the house, she wondered who might be at the door, she wasn't expecting anyone new today that might not know to just walk in.

On the porch was a short man with glasses, dark hair and a mustache that made her think of Hitler. He had a bulky envelope and a fancy clipboard in his hands. When she opened the door, he looked her over from head to toe and frowned.

"Can I help you?"

"Are you Carol Anderson?"

"Yes."

He frowned again. "May I see some ID please?"

She had no idea why he needed to see her identification,

but she decided to go along with it. "Would you like to come in while I go get it?"

He grimaced and shook his head. "No. I'll wait right here."

Stranger and stranger. As she retrieved her driver's license, she questioned whether she should show it to some unknown man.

The man was still standing exactly where she had left him, she wondered if he'd even blinked while she was gone. "I would like to see your identification as well, sir."

A card appeared so quickly it seemed like it was whipped out of thin air. "I am Joseph James Jenkinson and I represent the legal courier company Legal Eagle Deliveries. I have a package for you if you can prove you are Carol Anderson."

Carol had no idea who was sending her something legal, but she handed over her license. He carefully perused it and looked up and carefully examined her face. She felt this was getting rather ridiculous, but her curiosity held her steady.

He finally handed her ID back and held out the clipboard. "Sign here, please."

She did as she was told, and the man handed her the package. Then he turned around and marched down the sidewalk without another word. Carol wanted to laugh at the odd little man, but she knew that was not a nice reaction. So, she shut the door and took the package into the kitchen where she had left her glass of lemonade.

An hour later when Max walked into the kitchen, she was still sitting at the bar looking at the contents of the package. His arrival finally knocked her out of the stupor she felt. Her lemonade was a watery mess, still completely full. She hadn't taken a single sip.

Max said, "Hey, what's up? You look flummoxed."

"That's a very apt description. I have no idea what to do about this." She gestured toward the package contents.

Max looked at the items before her. "I see keys. Something that looks like a poem. A deed to something, a check-book, and a letter. So, what's it all about."

"It is a deed and keys to an old, abandoned house on the outskirts of town. The people who owned it moved to Phoenix about a dozen years ago, maybe more. Apparently, the last one died last week, and a courier was given the task of delivering this to me."

Max nodded. "That's simple enough. What else?"

"I'm supposed to turn it into a library for the city."

"Well, that might be some work if it's too rundown. Do you have the funds for something like that?"

She tapped the checkbook. "No, but they also gave me some money to do it. I'll need someone to look the house over. But the really strange part is the poem. I'm not exactly sure what it's alluding to."

Max picked up and read it.

"Little boy blue, we'll take you down,

To match the lady who is wearing the crown.

Where is the dragon that's guarding the keep?

Down in the basement, then oh so deep.

Treasures galore, so long ignored.

To be loved again, when all is restored."

Max set the paper down on the counter. "Sounds like gibberish to me."

"Yeah that's what I thought too. I've been thinking about it for a while and cannot come up with any reasonable conclusion."

"So just forget that for now, let's concentrate on the building. I can help you out with going to look at it. I've worked on some renovations for old houses."

Carol was thrilled he offered to go look at it with her. She had no knowledge in this area, and didn't want to pull their resident contractor, Marc, off the church's building project for this. "That's a very generous offer. Thank you."

"No problem. Do you want to go tomorrow after you get the breakfast taken care of?"

"Don't you need to be at the church?"

"No, not really. We covered a lot today. I'll text Marc to let him know. Then he can call if he needs me."

Carol knew the sooner she visited the place and got an idea of what would be needed, the better it would be. She'd been in it a time or two, many years ago, but had no idea what kind of shape it would be in now or if there was the remotest possibility of using it as the Zimmermans had asked. "If you're certain, tomorrow would be great. I've got some new people coming in for the weekend, so either tomorrow or I'll need to wait until Monday."

"Tomorrow it is then."

Relief flooded her. "Thanks, I appreciate it."

"My pleasure." He meant that, it would be a pleasure to spend the day with Carol. He grabbed one of his beers out of the fridge and went up to his room. He did have a couple of things he needed to do before he took the next day off.

Max was a little surprised at himself for volunteering to go with Carol. He didn't really like old houses and their renovations. His favorite was new buildings. But Carol had looked so lost, when he'd walked in, that he probably would have volunteered for about anything, to help ease her anxiety. This inheritance had thrown her for a loop.

The poem was just stupid, but it probably wouldn't hurt to take it along, or at least read it over again, just in case something struck him while they were in the house. He chose to take his measuring device, something he could easily do, to help her visualize how to turn it into a library, would be to draw up a good set of plans.

Max made a list of things they would want to take with them. Light sources being the first and foremost. He could ask her in the morning what she had on hand for that, and maybe run out to the camping outfitter they had in town, for tourists who opted to go hiking in the Cascades. He would have an hour or two after the stores opened while she was cleaning up the breakfast.

A few basic tools, some WD-40, and duct tape was always a welcome addition to scouting out an old house. There might be creatures inside also, so they might want to take some things with them to start the de-infestation.

He finished his list and dug into the work he needed to accomplish for the church.

Just as Max finished with the plan revisions for the church his phone buzzed. He pushed the talk button. "Well, hello brother of mine."

"Hey, Max. So, how's it going?"

"Great actually. Just worked on a couple of changes to the second floor, added some wiring to what will be the teen room. The music program has expanded to now include guitars, so they needed more juice."

"That's exactly why you're there."

"Yep. I'm going out with Carol Anderson tomorrow to check out an older house someone left to her to turn into a library."

"Not exactly your cup of tea. Want to trade places? The job I was working on lost their funding, so I'm free if you want me to take the older house."

"No, I'm fine with it, we're going out to it tomorrow to see what condition it's in. I'm going to take some measurements and see if I can draw her up a basic floor plan."

Wes chuckled. "I never thought I would see the day that you volunteered to go to an old house. Does Carol have some magic, or is she drugging you?"

"Neither, I'm just lending a hand. She's a nice woman."

"And gorgeous."

"Funny you never mentioned that."

Max could almost hear his brother's shrug. "Wasn't relative to the job."

"I suppose not, but it was a surprise nonetheless."

"Is that interest I hear in your voice, Brother?"

Max knew there probably was interest in his voice, but it was a futile interest. "No, we live too far apart."

"So, there is interest, but you're keeping it real?"

This was his twin, if he could talk to anyone, it would be Wes. "Yeah, I have to admit I wasn't sad to feel the spark. Showed me I hadn't let that part of me die with Jeanette."

"Damn shame about Jeanette, but I'm glad to hear that, too. No reason you couldn't extend your stay to enjoy the lovely widow."

"Nah, wouldn't be right."

"If you say so. Well let me know if you want me to come out for the old house. Have fun tomorrow. Make sure you wear work boots, in case of critter infestation."

Max snorted. "For sure. Give Kendra my love."

"Will do, later."

Max put the phone back on the desk. Did he want to hang around longer to spend more time with Carol? He knew he would certainly relish every minute, but no, it didn't seem right. He would help her with the initial assessment on the house, but they would keep it strictly business.

CHAPTER SIX

*E*xcitement warred with trepidation in Carol's thoughts, as she set out the breakfast buffet. She was excited to see what the old house looked like after so many years of sitting vacant, but why had the Zimmermans left *her* the house, rather than the city itself? She didn't know much about deeding a house to a city, maybe it didn't work that way at all, and they'd picked the remaining Anderson. Then again, she was mayor when they left, so maybe they just assumed she still would be.

Carol shrugged, she'd been thinking these same thoughts since the moment she'd opened the package. It was silly to be going over and over the same questions. She would simply go out there with Max and see what there was to see.

She'd donned jeans, sturdy boots, and a long-sleeved t-shirt. The long sleeves might make her sweaty when the temperature rose, but she wanted her arms covered in case of spiders, or anything else, for that matter. Before she left to go, she would contain her hair, so it had less chance of getting nasty in the old house.

Carol greeted her guests as they came in for breakfast.

She had a good group currently, a nice mix of people and family sizes. Several of them would be leaving on Saturday morning with new people arriving on the ferry. It made the weekend hectic, but such was the nature of the beast, most of her turn-overs were on the weekend.

Max came in with a notebook in his hand, laid it on the table and filled a plate and coffee mug. Carol went over to his table once he was seated. "Are we still on for today?"

"Yes. I wanted to see if you had a few things, can you join me for a minute?"

"Sure, let me check the buffet and grab a cup of coffee."

When she'd joined him at his table, he opened the notebook to a list.

Max gestured toward the notebook. "I thought we should take these with us today. So, if you have them, great. If you don't, I'll run out and get them while you clean up the breakfast."

Carol was a little surprised at the thoroughness of the list. She had a lot of the items, but had not considered taking them with them to go look at the house. A lot of them made sense and when he explained his reasoning on the others, she understood the suggestions.

The man had really thought this through. She'd decided they needed some of those items and knew she had them on hand. But Max had gone far beyond her and she was grateful for him offering to go with her.

Standing to refill the buffet, she said, "That's a very impressive list, some things will be at the general store, for the others, check the outfitters on the next street over, they often have random things. Tell them to put it on my tab."

"But they don't know me, why would they believe me?"

"They already know who you are, what you're doing here in town, that you're staying at my B&B, but never fear, if they don't believe you, they will call me to verify."

Max shook his head. "Small towns never cease to amaze me."

She just laughed at him. "Big city boy." Then walked away grinning.

Max found everything that he'd wanted to take out to the house. He'd had no trouble at all putting the items he purchased on Carol's tab. She was right, everyone knew all about his personal and professional business. He'd been more than a little surprised when both shop owners had called him by name and asked how the church building was coming along. A couple of other people walking down the street greeted him, by name as well. It was a little freaky.

When he got back to the B&B Carol was ready for him. Adorable was the only word that came to mind when he saw her. She'd pulled her hair into a bun, and had on old clothes that would be perfect for tramping around in some dusty old house.

Her eyes, however, were shining with excitement, and she had supplies loaded into a large tote. He was drawn to that excitement and felt the same sentiment rise up in him. His brother would have laughed out loud at his eagerness to get out to that old house and explore.

Max couldn't tell if the house really did interest him, or if it was all because of Carol's enthusiasm. He knew the place might be a wreck, but he was still ready and willing to go find out. Eventually, someone would need to go up on the roof to see what shape it was in. But not today.

He asked, "You ready?"

"I am, it's kind of close to lunch, should we take something with us, or stop somewhere?"

Max felt an impatience to get going and didn't want to

think about food, but he didn't want to be foolish, it was a valid concern, so he considered his answer. "Good question. I would say let's eat after, but we will probably be filthy. Maybe some granola bars would be good to take along and some bottles of water, for now. After, we could order a pizza or something while we shower and change."

"I'll get some water and power bars, while you load the car." Carol handed him the keys and he gathered up all their gear. He had to admit he'd been a little surprised at her choice of vehicles. The Outback was a few years old, but in good condition, he wondered how often she needed the four-wheel drive. Max packed all the supplies in the cargo area and went back into the house to see if she needed more help.

Carol had prepared a little cooler with water and another bag with snacks. She'd also filled up an old milk jug with water and had a roll of paper towels.

Max nodded at the water. "Good idea. That might come in handy."

Carol pulled up to the enormous wrought iron gate with a padlock on it. A fence of the same design spread out in both directions. He couldn't see the house from the gate, which was a little frustrating. The padlock was old and large, would it even work after so many years in the weather? They exchanged glances and then they both got out of the car to see about getting the padlock off. He grabbed the WD-40 and she had the keys. He doused the lock with plenty of lubricant and they both waited impatiently for it to do its job.

The first try didn't work, so they doused the lock a second time and let it penetrate. That time there was a tiny bit of movement. So, they worked the key back and forth to help spread the oil.

SHIRLEY PENICK

"If we can't get it open. We could always cut it off. I imagine the fire department has bolt cutters."

Carol nodded as she kept up working the key back and forth. "They do. But then we would have to wait to get them. I'm too impatient for that. Give it one more squirt, it's moving more."

Max could agree with not wanting to wait, he felt excitement building and he didn't want to disappoint Carol. She was nearly vibrating with eagerness. They waited a third time.

He asked, "Want me to give it a try?"

"Sure, but finesse it, don't break the key hulking it off."

"Got it, no superhuman strength." Max chuckled and started turning the key back and forth. He could feel it give a smidgeon with each rotation of the key. Finally, it did turn all the way, but the hasp didn't pop loose.

"I think the key is in the open place. Hold it in that spot and let me see if I can yank on the hasp a bit."

Carol's fingers brushed his as she took hold of the key to keep it in the unlocked position. Her touch sent sparks up his arm, but he refused to be side-tracked. He yanked on the hasp a couple of times until it opened, and then he had to force it to turn. The next time he went to an old house, he was bringing bolt cutters. They had been mucking around with the darn lock for nearly a half hour.

CHAPTER SEVEN

*C*arol was elated when Max got the lock fully opened. She'd never considered having trouble getting through the gate. If Max hadn't come with her, she was not certain she would have remembered to bring the lubricant.

They wiped their oily hands on some paper towels and headed up the driveway. The yard was so overgrown it was nearly a jungle. There were a couple of trees leaning precariously over the driveway, but she had enough room to maneuver past them. It was something to add to the list of what was needed to use the building. Maybe she could have the town do a work day. Providing any of this was viable, at all.

After passing all the trees the house rose up before them. She stopped the car in the drive so they could take it all in. It was larger than she remembered, but she'd only been out a few times and mostly at night. In the daytime it looked much different and she realized the Zimmermans had probably only had the essential areas lit when she'd come out years ago.

The design was similar to her house, with the wrap-around porch, asymmetrical façade, and dominant front facing gable. Where it differed from hers were all the towers, she could see three from the car, the central tower was massive rising easily four stories. She wondered if it had been a bell tower.

All the windows were boarded up, which might have saved the glass, but it was going to be pitch dark in the house, until she got someone with a ladder out here to remove the boards. She didn't want to turn the electricity on until it was inspected, both in the house and leading to it from the last part of town. It was a good thing Max had insisted on getting some battery-operated lanterns.

Max said, "It's not a house, it's a mansion. Queen Anne Victorian, like your house, but on a much grander scale. There looks to be at least four balconies and look at that huge tower. Was this once the city hall or something? I don't know why else they would need a bell tower, or maybe it was a clock tower."

"I have no idea. I didn't realize it was so large. I can't imagine a library for our little town filling it."

"There could be some meeting rooms maybe. Typically, the floor plans for these houses have little alcoves that could be used as reading nooks. Some of the smaller rooms might be suitable for reading groups or activities. We'll have to see what the inside is like. How the rooms can be arranged or remodeled. Let's start with a walk around the house. I want to take some measurements to see if I can draw you up a set of floor plans."

"That would be helpful. They might have some filed with the city. If they did any renovations." Carol shrugged. She knew that in some ways the town had run efficiently and in some ways it had not. She had no idea how the town planning and zoning had handled things before she became mayor.

Her husband had been the mayor for a few years before his death, but she didn't know what records he had kept. They'd talked about city business a lot, which was why she could step into the mayoral role, but all the details, like record keeping, hadn't been topics of conversation. And she had no idea what her father-in-law might have done. "It's hard to say."

"Well, I can get you started, and you can check with the town records tomorrow or whenever you have time."

Carol pulled her car alongside the house and parked it in a relatively open area. Everything was overgrown, even what had been the gravel driveway and parking areas had plants encroaching. Dear God, just the grounds were going to take a massive effort to tame. Carol wanted to turn around and go straight home. This idea was ridiculous. But she'd never backed down from a challenge before and she wasn't about to start now. She had to at least access the building to see if it was sound.

It might be easier to just tear the thing down and build a new building. But that was not what the Zimmermans had wanted, so she had to at least try. She would do her due diligence and give the idea a fair chance. If it wasn't feasible then she would make a plan B.

Max got out one door and she followed him. Taking a walk around the building would give her more information and then they could work on getting inside. At least the front door had a porch over it, so maybe the lock would be in better condition.

Max was surprised at how excited he felt about exploring the old mansion. And it wasn't just to help out the pretty lady. No, he felt an odd attraction to this place that he rarely had with older buildings. The grounds were a mess and cleaning them up would be a significant job, but he just let that information slide past as he focused on the structure, itching to see how the interior was laid out.

First things first and that was to do the walk around. That would give them an idea of how many doors the building had, if there was any underground storage, like a root cellar, and if the windows and doors were intact. Which would be valuable information for when they got inside.

The overgrown grounds made the walk around the perimeter of the house challenging. Plants that should have been cute little bushes had grown into trees. The flower beds were mostly weeds, all the flowers strangled out years ago. From his glimpses between the foliage, the foundation looked sound.

He took measurements along two sides and when they got to the rear of the house things got more interesting. There were two doors, one that looked to be off the kitchen, since there was what used to be a kitchen garden. The rosemary was over four feet tall, the thyme had filled in every spot on the ground it could. Further back were corn and giant tomato plants, there was a mound of either cucumbers or zucchini, or maybe both. One side sported several large grape arbors, since grapes grew well in the area, it wasn't a surprise that they were thriving. In the distance were trees, that were most likely apples.

Carol turned to him her eyes shining with enthusiasm. "Do you see this garden? It's huge. Overgrown like crazy, but it's got nearly everything that can be grown. I didn't know rosemary grew that tall. Did you?"

Max was cold-cocked by her expression, his heart pounded and all he could think of was kissing her senseless. He clenched his fist to avoid temptation and pointed to the trees in the distance. "Apples or peaches."

"Maybe both."

While she was distracted, he continued on. Distance from the lovely woman would be a good thing. Not far from the door was a root cellar, the covering trapped under some kind of vine that looked like a weed, but might be some kind of food, with its proximity to the kitchen garden. They would explore that later.

Carol walked up next to him, but as she got near, her foot caught on the vine covering the root cellar and she squawked. He turned to catch her before she fell, his hands dropping everything. He grabbed her by the arms as she plowed into him.

Max's body started to respond to the lovely bit of femininity in his arms, he had to move quick, or she might notice. He quickly stepped back away from her, making certain she was steady on her feet, then bent to gather his belongings. Nothing was damaged. He'd dropped the laser measuring device more than once in the past and now had it protected by a heavy-duty case.

Carol stood there for a moment her eyes round from the near fall. She muttered, "Thanks."

He nodded jerkily, still trying to reign in his wayward body. "You're welcome."

Max moved forward. That was a close call and Max hoped there wouldn't be any more of those.

Further along was a door that he assumed was the back entrance to the house, whether it led to a mud room or a parlor he wouldn't know until they got inside. He really had expected to find a door that would be for servant stairs, but he hadn't seen one. Maybe the door to the kitchen led off to that access. Unusual but not unheard of.

The porch started up as they turned the last corner and ran the full distance to the front door. There were steps on this side also, so rather than fighting the foliage he led the way up onto the porch. The stone steps were cracked and broken in places, washed away, and Max figured they would need repair or replacement. He'd not noticed that on the main stairs in front, so maybe they had been repaired in the past.

They were back at the front door. So, he put his measuring device down. "I'll go get the rest of our supplies; you see if you can figure out which key fits the door."

He left Carol and hurried back to the car. The inside of the house should be safer than the grounds. Darker, but safer.

CHAPTER EIGHT

The front door opened much easier than the gate had. It still needed a squirt or two of WD-40, but the key turned easily, and the hinges only creaked a little.

Max chuckled. "It sounds like a haunted house, just as much as it looks like one."

Carol liked the sound of his easy chuckle, it filled her heart with warmth, and she wondered about the slight yearning she felt. The companionship she had with Max was different than with the other men she knew. Maybe it was just the similar age, most of the other men in her sphere were younger than she was or married. It was nice to enjoy the sound, but that's as far as it was going to go.

After all, he'd practically pushed her away earlier when she'd tripped. She'd been glad for his help, she'd already had one surgery from falling, she didn't need another one. But while she'd felt safe and secure in his arms, he'd obviously not felt the same. Which was fine. They needed to keep this business only. Even if her feminine self was a little miffed at his reaction. No, it was better this way. No cozy embraces. No stolen kisses.

She said, "I imagine the librarians will have a field day in the month of October, providing we can pull this idea off."

"Well let's go in and find out, shall we?" Max leaned down and grabbed their supplies from the porch.

Carol took one of the flashlights and turned it on. Shining it into the room in front of them, she took her first few cautious steps in the door. There were cobwebs everywhere, sweeping down from the ceiling in huge swaths. A few industrious spiders held court in the corners. The air was stale and still, which might be a good thing, indicating that the house wasn't open to the elements.

Max followed her in, bouncing a little as he walked, she didn't feel any give, even with the large man testing the floor.

"It's musty smelling, that's a good sign. We should have brought a candle, they are the best indicators of airflow," Max said echoing her thoughts.

"I have a lighter in the car so if we find a candle, we can light it."

"Good to know."

They went from room to room, in what seemed like a maze to her. The rooms were mostly empty, only a few scattered pieces of old furniture remained. There were cobwebs and spiderwebs, but they didn't encounter any mice or rats, which surprised her. She had expected some, maybe even some bats up on the top floor.

She wandered along with Max as he measured and took notes. She would be interested to see what the floor plan really looked like. She was totally turned around and with the windows boarded up she had no point of reference. Just about the time she decided they would be lost in the maze of rooms forever, they arrived back in the foyer with the stairs.

They'd found the kitchen and a large parlor that had the doors they'd seen from the outside. But they'd never seen any servant stairs, she was surprised by that, even her house had a second set of stairs that led between the kitchen and the second and third floors. Her stairs were narrow and steep, so she avoided them. She'd thought about locking them, but that wouldn't be safe and would be against the fire code.

Max interrupted her thoughts. "Quite the warren of rooms."

"Yeah, I was beginning to wonder if we should have left breadcrumbs."

Max chuckled. She did enjoy that man's chuckle. What would his full laugh be like?

"Until we determine the vermin population, I don't think that would be wise. Maybe a ball of string would work."

"I think string would get tangled and we'd get even more lost."

His eyes danced with humor which made her belly clench. She silently told her body to behave. She was not going down that path. So, it was futile, besides that, she hadn't had feelings like this since her husband had died and she didn't need them to start now. She was in her fifties for goodness sake, she wasn't a teenager anymore.

"You might be right about that."

Right about what? What had they been talking about? Her busy mind had gone off on a tangent. Good grief, she wasn't senile. No sir, just infatuated by the man standing next to her.

"So, are you ready to try the next floor? Bedrooms should be a little less chaotic than the main floor."

Oh, yes, now she remembered, string and breadcrumbs, and which would be best to find their way through the maze. "We can hope."

~

41

Max stopped in shock and did a double take. "I thought it would be less chaotic up here, obviously I was wrong. This upper floor is laid out in a most unusual fashion. I thought there would be a central hall with other halls leading to the wings." He frowned at the two parallel halls with larger rooms on the outside walls and smaller rooms on the inside. It was a most peculiar setup.

Carol muttered, "It's kind of crazy. Whoever designed this house must have been on drugs."

Max couldn't deny her observation. "I agree it is different. Maybe the owners wanted something unique. My brother and I have had some strange requests. People wanting 'something different' which is hard to do and still make it livable."

Carol shook her head as they turned yet another corner. "Something different. Well, they got that in spades. The towers are more obvious on this floor, they are those large corner rooms."

"Yes, I think so. It might take me a couple of days to get this drawn up. I wasn't expecting anything quite so elaborate."

"There's no rush. It's not going anywhere."

The house wasn't going anywhere, but he wasn't planning to stay indefinitely in this small town. He wanted to get the current floor plan drawn up, so he could give her some good ideas for the remodel. "No, I suppose not."

The third floor was not quite as confusing as the other two. This was clearly the servant's quarters; the rooms were very small. After they were done with that floor Max stopped and looked around. "Did you see any door that might lead to the bell or clock tower?"

Carol cocked her head to the side. "No, I didn't, but there has to be a door somewhere. And we still haven't found the servant stairs. This house is really weird."

"I couldn't agree more. Maybe when I draw up the rooms, we'll see where everything should be."

"Boy, I wouldn't want that job for all the tea in China." Carol shuddered dramatically, which made Max chuckle at her.

"We'll have to come back to find the door to the tower. I assume the lower levels are incorporated into the living space but there still should be access somewhere for the fourth floor. It might be a pull-down ladder that we didn't see in the dark. I don't want to search for it now, I think it's getting late. We can't tell from here, but I'll bet it's close to dark."

Carol pulled out her phone. "Oh, you're right. We should get going, we've been in here for hours."

"Do you want to put that old lock back on the gate?"

"No, I don't think anyone is going to break in. We can lock the building, and maybe pull the gates shut, but I don't trust that old lock. I'll go pick up a new one, which isn't going to rust shut immediately."

"Sounds good, let's get moving. I didn't realize it earlier, but I'm getting a touch on the hungry side." Max started down the stairs.

Carol ran her hand down the balustrade. "I'd like to see this in a better light than what the flashlights and lanterns gave off. I'm hungry too. What kind of pizza do you want?"

"Anything. From cheese only to fully loaded. Taking the boards off the windows would help."

"I was thinking fully loaded tonight since we never had lunch. Those granola bars only do so much. Maybe I can get Terry and Greg to pull the boards over the windows down, at least on the first floor. After all what are sons and sons-in-law for anyway?"

Max chuckled; the woman cracked him up. He'd not met

either of the men she was talking about. They weren't part of the church building project. Although she'd pointed out Greg's bar and he'd heard Terry worked with wood to create fine furniture. "Good to know they are good for something."

CHAPTER NINE

$\mathcal{M}$ ax had been working on the plans of the old mansion for a couple of days and things just weren't adding up. Either he'd gotten the measurements wrong, or they had missed a large chunk of the house. There seemed to be a large rectangular section missing in the middle of the house. He'd never seen anything like it. At least not in modern times.

If he'd been studying castles from medieval Europe he wouldn't have been surprised in the least. Some form of tennazzi or donjon, sometimes referred to as a keep, was often found in those days. But what would be the purpose of something like that in today's modern world? Even in the Victorian era, unless someone was afraid of some kind of uprising, he couldn't figure out the purpose.

Max supposed the only answer would be to go back to the house and do more investigation. He'd worked on it all weekend and come up with missing space on each floor. Maybe he'd been wrong about the tower and *it* was the missing space. If that was the case, they'd missed a door.

He kept thinking about it as he went to find Carol. The

poem popped into his head, there had been something about a dragon guarding the keep. But before they went down that rabbit hole, he wanted to look at the house with more light. Carol had said she'd asked Greg and Terry to take down the boards over the windows. If they'd gotten that done it would help a lot.

Carol wasn't in any of the common areas, or outside. Her car was in the back, not that she couldn't have walked somewhere, but he had the feeling she was near. He didn't know if it was proper to knock on her bedroom door, but he wanted to get some plans made before returning to the house, and didn't want to wait until morning. She'd mentioned being able to go out on Monday, which was tomorrow, so if she was free then he wanted to get it set up. then he could text Marc to see if they needed him.

Max found her room on the second floor and rapped on the door. He heard a flurry of movement, and Carol called out that she would be right there.

When she opened the door, he nearly swallowed his tongue. She was belting a silk crimson colored short robe around her still damp body, her hair up in a towel. He'd disturbed her shower, or after shower. The robe was happily absorbing water and clinging to her body, giving him a very good view of her curves.

"What is it? What's wrong? Do we need to call the fire department?"

Dammit, he'd scared the shit out of her. He swallowed to try to get some moisture going in his mouth so he could speak, even then his voice croaked when he spoke. "No, I'm sorry I didn't mean to startle you, there is no problem I just wanted to talk to you. It never occurred to me…" He waived in her direction, no more words came to his rescue and he just stood there mute, like a dumbass.

Carol's heart was pumping madly, adrenaline had shot through her at the knock on her door. No one ever came to her door except for emergencies. "There's no emergency?"

Max shook his head and growled out, "No."

Relief shot through her, she could count on one hand the number of times someone had searched for her and found her in her room. Once an older man was having heart trouble, she'd called the town dispatcher who had gotten the fire department and the doctor here in short order. They had transported him to the clinic and the doctor had gotten him stabilized for the helicopter trip to Chelan, and the hospital there. Another time a child had hurt himself and needed a Band-Aid, the young mother had panicked and couldn't remember where the first aid kit was, the husband nearly as wild-eyed as the mom. She couldn't remember a time where someone had knocked on her door just to talk.

Carol frowned at Max. He'd scared the crap out of her for no reason. "I was in the shower, well, just out of it. I don't have the time or energy in the morning, so once all my guests are out doing touristy stuff that's when I have the time. What do you need?"

Max cleared his throat and looked around madly. "I can't remember. How about you finish getting dressed and I'll meet you downstairs somewhere."

What was wrong with him? Was he having a stroke or something? His color looked fine and there were no other warning signs apparent, just confusion. It might be good to keep an eye on him. "I was going to take a glass of white wine out on the back deck and watch the sunset."

He nodded. "I'll pour and meet you out there." He pivoted and walked away, Carol watched him go for a moment and then went back inside.

She saw herself in the mirror and it hit her. Her mini-robe that she'd flung on barely covered her, what it did cover had dampened the robe to where it clung to her boobs and ass. She'd belted it but not gotten it closed on top very well, so there was a lot of skin showing. Maybe his confusion was just plain old lust. She'd not turned a man stupid in a hell of a long time. Her face was positively smug, with a touch of wicked.

CHAPTER TEN

*M*ax poured a glass of wine for Carol and grabbed a beer for himself. He'd just acted like the world's biggest idiot. When Carol had appeared in that door, every drop of blood in his body had headed south, and he couldn't move, couldn't breathe, couldn't think. So, he'd just stood there like a moron. He wondered if his mouth had been opening and closing like some sort of demented fish.

As soon as he'd gotten out of the danger zone, the blood had returned to his head and he could remember why he'd gone to her door in the first place. So now he just had to get the picture of her standing there looking so damn sexy out of his head, so he could speak to her like an intelligent human being.

He sipped his beer and waited for her to appear, sunset was a while off, so he wondered if she'd really been planning to sit out here for that long. Maybe it had been the only thing that had popped into her head while he was being the demented fish. He shook his head at his own foolishness.

Maybe he needed a girlfriend. He would think about that when he got back home.

Carol strolled out onto the deck, bringing the lust right back into his body. He was prepared this time and wasn't going to let it affect him. He wasn't a teenager and didn't need to think with his dick.

Then he looked at her and knew all hope was lost. She had on some sort of floaty dress thing that reached her ankles and swirled around her as she walked. Her hair was still damp and curling around her face, making love to her shoulders, lucky hair. Her eyes held a wicked light that let him know she was aware of his attraction. Then she banked that wickedness and returned to professional.

Damn, he kind of liked the wicked. Then again, if he was going to get through this discussion, he needed to be able to think. But it was still a shame, he could almost bet she didn't let anyone else see that wicked expression, even for a moment.

Carol picked up her wine from the table and sat in the other lounger. She took a drink from her glass, looking toward where the sun would set in an hour or so. God, she was beautiful.

Without turning toward him, she asked, "So, what did you want to talk about?"

He cleared his throat and hoped it would clear his head too. "The house. The measurements I took inside don't line up with the outside."

"What do you mean?"

"There is a large area in the middle that is a void."

Carol turned toward him, a frown marring her brow. "How could that be?"

"We missed something. I don't know how we missed it, but we did."

"Do you think it's the tower? How big is the void?"

"Big, Twenty-five by fifty feet."

"No, that's ridiculous."

"I agree, which is why I was thinking about going back out again tomorrow. I thought we could search the rooms for a door."

Carol clapped her hands together, her eyes sparkling with excitement. "How fun, let's do it."

He tried to ignore the enthusiasm beaming from the woman. He had to work to keep some of the blood in his head so he could think. "Did Terry and Greg get the boards off the windows? I'm assuming we need more light, and that's why we missed it the first time."

"They did. Greg made it into a training mission for the fire department. They took the ladder truck out, removed the boards, and even checked the roof. Terry said the roof is tile, so it's in much better shape than he thought it would be. There were a few broken tiles, so they put some plastic over those areas, but for the most part they said it was very secure."

"Excellent. The other thing you need to do as soon as possible is get an electrician out to check out the wiring."

"Our only town electrician is working on the church and I don't want to derail that for this project, so we'll have to use lanterns and candles for the time being."

He shook his head. "Of course. I'm not used to living in a place where there is only one electrician."

She laughed. "Technically there are two, but they are both in the same company and working on the church to get it done on time."

Carol was excited by the idea of a secret room. It would be huge, unless of course, it was also a maze of rooms. She'd checked with the city and they said there were no plans on file for the house. Which seemed odd to her, the Zimmermans had been gone less than twenty years. Why wouldn't there be plans on file?

"So, can you take tomorrow off? I could go on Tuesday if that won't work."

"I'll call Marc and ask him. When I checked in Friday night, he said he didn't anticipate needing me for anything."

Carol wondered how long Max would stay in town if Marc didn't need him anymore. But she didn't want to ask that question for some odd reason. The house seemed to intrigue him enough for now, so she would just wait and see. She'd booked him into the room for a month, so she didn't have to worry about shuffling people around. And truth be told she didn't book that room too often, she still kind of thought of it as hers. Silly of her maybe, but true.

"All right let's plan on tomorrow. But I think I'll pack us a lunch this time, no point in getting hungry or hangry."

Max chuckled. "Sounds good, it's a good thing neither of us have blood sugar problems."

"Yes, it is. Getting old is not for the faint of heart."

A cloud passed through his eyes, quick and fleeting, but still there. "Better than the alternative."

Change of topic time. "Yes. So, are you a Mariner fan? They won last night in a double header."

"Yes, they were both great games. Did you watch them?" he asked, sounding surprised.

She grinned. "I am totally a closet baseball fanatic. I try not to miss a game."

They talked about baseball as the sun slowly sank behind the mountains and the light vanished. She had little lights on the deck and along all the walks that came on automatically when it got dark. The lights in the house did the same thing so her B&B was always warm and welcoming, even when she was busy, or not at home. She didn't want anyone stumbling around in the dark.

Neither she nor Max seemed in any hurry to part ways. They talked about other sports and hobbies they both enjoyed.

Max grinned. "You like hitting a bucket of balls at a driving range? That surprises me some."

She fiddled with her skirt hem, smoothing it out. She was having so much fun chatting with Max, he was good company, and the fact that his eyes followed her movements in a slightly hungry manor didn't hurt her feelings. In fact, his attention made her feel sexy. "I do. Real golf takes a lot more concentration and precision. But whacking a ball to see how far it can go is fun."

Music was the next conversation. He'd already caught her listening to Aerosmith so he knew she liked heavy rock. He liked more traditional rock but didn't mind the heavier stuff. He also surprised her when he said he liked opera.

"Really? Opera? Have you been to a lot of it?"

"Enough. I like it in person. The energy of the crowd. The soaring notes. It's all fascinating. I'm not sure I would be a fan if I wasn't in the audience, like on TV. It's a great experience in person."

"I've not been to a real opera. We've got a singing company in Chelan that performs, but it's not the same."

"That's a shame. You should come to the city and I'll take you to one."

Carol didn't think that would ever happen, her life was here in their little town, but it was a nice offer. "I'll see about that."

They talked until it got late and then reluctantly parted

ways for the night. She locked up knowing her guests had all gotten back.

She'd had such a pleasant evening with the man. Carol hoped they could have a few more like that before he returned to his home.

CHAPTER ELEVEN

*C*arol unlocked the door on the old house easily this time. No lubricant was needed. She stepped into the foyer, and reveled in the natural light that filled the place. It was wonderful to be able to see what the room really looked like. Of course, that also showed her how much work they would need to do.

The old wallpaper was faded and buckling at the seams. The chandelier was magnificent but draped in cobwebs and dust, several of the glass ornaments were missing or broken. The floors needed refinishing, some places were rough with splinters and would need significant sanding. The drapes hung next to the windows in limp threadbare fashion. The scattered furniture was broken and filthy. That was just the foyer.

Carol sighed and found one table that looked sturdy enough to hold their lunch and set it down gingerly, making sure it didn't collapse before setting the cooler and the keys next to it.

Max carted in their supplies, which had been added to

since their last visit, and this time he wore a backpack. Carol was curious as to the contents of the backpack, but she would just wait to see what he produced.

Max said, "Well it's nice to have light, but it sure does point out the flaws."

"I was thinking the same thing, and this is just one room." She sighed and continued, "I'm thinking that restoring this place is going to take years."

"But the whole thing would not have to be restored before you could open it as a library. The top floors could easily wait until they were needed."

Carol felt a bit of hope soar at that statement. It was true they wouldn't have to do the full thing right away. The main floor had more than enough space. A lot of it was all crammed up into smaller rooms, but there were a few larger areas. And maybe Max could help her figure it all out, before he left. "That's true. I think we should concentrate on that idea. We can certainly assess the whole place, but then put some of the work aside for later. A good cleaning of all three floors would be a good first step."

"It would, so for now, think about what you would want done on this floor in order to begin a library for the town."

"I will, let's get to investigating."

Max set his backpack down on the floor, next to their supplies, and unzipped it. He pulled a tablet out of it and she saw the laser measuring device was also in the bag, with spiral notebooks and a sketch book. After tapping around for a moment, he turned the screen toward her.

"Here is what I have drawn up. Do you see this big empty area? That is what we are looking for. I highlighted the walls we need to search to find the entrance."

"Oh, well that does help, doesn't it?"

"Hopefully. We are here." He pointed at the screen, where

an image of the first floor of the plans he'd created was displayed.

Carol could see the doors and windows to their back and the stairs in front of them. "This room doesn't share a wall."

"No, it's off to the side. The Victorian builders liked asymmetry. So, the front door is really off to one side, with just a small room on the right."

"We can look at that later to see what it needs, let's start to the left and see if we can find the door to the void."

Max chuckled. "The void, I like it." He handed her a flashlight and they started their investigation.

An hour and a half later they were back in the foyer, and had found no doors on the walls abutting the void. Max was perplexed, he'd checked his measurements and they were accurate. He reached into the cooler and handed Carol a bottle of water. "Well, that was frustrating."

"I agree. How can there be no access?"

"It could be on one of the other floors."

"What with a ladder or secret staircase. That sounds kind of silly."

Max chugged half of his water. "True... but having the void in the first place is kind of silly."

Carol opened her container of lunch food and brought out two bags of trail mix and two packets of wet wipes. Absently, she handed one of each to Max, her mind far away from what she was doing.

Max took the wipes and cleaned his hands, laying the spent wipe and its wrapper on the table. Carol pulled a trash bag out of the supplies, tossed her wipe in, then picked up his off the table and froze. "Where are the keys?"

"What keys?"

"The keys to the house. I laid them right here next to the food."

"Are you sure?"

She patted down her pockets and then looked in the food bag and the cooler. He sifted through their supplies and found nothing.

With a frown marring her pretty face she said, "I am sure. I don't see them anywhere else, do you?"

"No. Are you sure you didn't take them with you."

The frown deepened. "I don't think so. I remember setting them down here, but I don't remember picking them back up. I think all I was carrying was the water and the flashlight. They aren't in your backpack, are they?"

Max quickly pulled his backpack off and looked through it, he didn't remember picking them up, but anything was possible. He searched through it and found only what he'd put in there this morning.

"Nope, nothing in there that doesn't belong. Let's continue upstairs. I'm sure they're in one of the rooms down here, but I don't want to lose the light before we examine the floors above. We can always look for the keys before we leave. I'm sure we'll find them on a table in one of the rooms or maybe they fell out of your pocket."

She raised an eyebrow at him.

He looked at the tight jeans that showed off her very fine ass and chuckled. "Ok maybe not fell out of the pocket of your painted-on jeans."

Carol looked gratified as he tried to tear his gaze off her figure. She nodded. "I agree though, let's carry on with our investigation of the upper floors. It's not like we need the keys at this moment, and I heard it might storm this afternoon."

Max looked out the grimy window near him at the crystal-clear blue sky and bright sunlight. "If you say so."

Carol followed his gaze and then shrugged. "It could happen."

Max finished his trail mix, guzzled the rest of his water and put all the trash in the trash bag. "Ready?"

She tossed her trash in and picked up her flashlight. "Let's do this thing."

CHAPTER TWELVE

$\mathscr{C}$arol followed Max as they went up the stairs to examine the second story. Her mind still pondering where those damn keys had gotten to. She was ninety nine percent sure she'd left them on that table. But they couldn't just get up and walk off. She didn't think there were any critters in the house. She'd heard raccoons liked shiny things and of course jay birds. But it seemed like if either of those animals were in the house there would be evidence of them, in the form of poop, at the very least. They'd seen nothing like that, on the first floor anyway.

When they started on the second floor, they searched the walls that would share a side with the void, but again found nothing. Max had taken to muttering as he measured, and she wondered if he was feeling as frustrated as she was.

She stilled and said, "Did you hear that?"

Max looked up with a blank expression. "Hear what?"

"I just thought I heard a door close."

"Did you tell someone you were coming out today? Maybe it's one of them."

She'd mentioned the project to her kids, and might have

said something about today's visit, but none of them had expressed any interest in joining her in the search. "Yeah, a few people, but I think they would text first before coming out."

"Do we have reception out here?"

Carol pulled out her phone. There was reception, but it was weak. "A little."

"We're just two rooms from the staircase, go ahead and go over to the landing, so you can call out and tell them we're upstairs."

Carol walked out of the room and around the corner to the stairs. "Terry? Greg? Who's there?"

Silence answered her.

"Hello?"

More silence. Frustrated, and maybe a little spooked, she returned to the room Max had moved to. "No one answered."

"Maybe it was a tree hitting the side of the house or a loose shutter."

The window did show there was a breeze outside. Not a huge one, but she supposed it could have caused the noise. It had sounded like a door though, not just random banging. Was her imagination running away with her?

Max turned away from his measuring, frustration vibrating in his voice. "No changes and still no access to the void. I just don't get it."

"We'll figure it out. Do you want to stop for a while and have lunch, then we can do the final floor?"

His stomach growled on cue. Carol laughed. Max gave her a crooked smile, that did something warm to her insides. "I guess we're having lunch."

Carol handed out another wet wipe and used one herself. Then she handed Max a sandwich and a bag of cut-up veggies. She picked up her own sandwich and stared into the bag, dumbfounded. The keys were laying in the bottom of the bag. She pulled them out and shook them at Max.

"The keys were in the lunch bag?" Max asked.

"Yes. But I checked it earlier and they weren't."

"Are you sure?"

Carol felt like she was losing her mind. She'd left them on the table, she was sure of it. Then when she'd discovered they were missing she'd checked the bag, even though she hadn't opened it until she got the trail mix out. And now they were in that same bag, under her sandwich. She sure as hell didn't pull out her sandwich to hide the keys under it.

"I'm either losing my mind or we have ghosts."

Max's eyes twinkled with mirth. "Ah, blaming it on the poltergeist. Always a great idea. Or maybe it's a house elf that someone left behind, and it's ticked off."

Carol giggled at his teasing. She put the conundrum far behind her to think about later. Max was looking at her, mischief in his eyes, the rest of him oozing sex appeal. It was either laugh or jump the man, the teasing twinkle in his eyes drew her in like a moth to a flame. Better to pass it off, with a laugh, than get burned.

Max ate his delicious lunch and tried to ignore his ever-growing interest in Carol Anderson. She was a delight. He'd felt something from her when he'd teased her about a house elf hiding their keys. But she'd drawn back and hidden whatever it was. He'd give a lot to know what she'd been thinking for that moment in time. He couldn't come right out and ask, so he forced the thought away.

Carol said, "All kidding aside, that keys thing is weird."

Max nodded slowly, thinking, he couldn't figure out the keys any more than he could the void. However, he figured the enormous mystery of the room was more important than the keys. But he was going to put them in his pockets or backpack when they went up to the last floor. "Yeah. I'll put them in my pocket when we do the top floor. We've got a couple of mysteries going on, I'd be the most happy to solve the missing space one."

"I agree, keys and closing doors is nothing compared to a thousand square feet missing on three floors."

"And possibly the fourth also."

Her gaze met his with a startled expression in her eyes. "That would kind of make sense." She wiped her hands and balled up the trash. "Well, we better get going before that storm hits."

Max looked out the window again to find clear blue skies and bright sunshine, the wind was gusting a little stronger than it had been, but there were no clouds in the sky. He didn't comment, just pocketed the keys and threw his trash in the bag. "Great lunch. Thanks."

"You're welcome. I packed cookies to celebrate finding the void."

"Oh man. Do we still get to eat them even if we don't find it?"

"I suppose. It never occurred to me we wouldn't find it."

"Yeah I totally thought we'd just overlooked it in the dark and would spot it right away and laugh at ourselves for missing it. But..." He trailed off with a shrug.

"Maybe we'll still do that, we've got one more floor to search."

He was beginning to lose hope on that front, but he picked up his backpack and his flashlight and followed Carol up the stairs, and suddenly wished he'd gone first. The tight jeans showed off a great ass and short, but firm, legs. He bit back a groan and thought about surging past her. That would make him look like an idiot, so he decided to just enjoy the sight. It wasn't likely to be a repeated event, so he might as well appreciate it while he had the chance.

They searched the third floor and found nothing. Max noticed it was a lot darker on this top floor, but he just kept moving from one little room to another. It was positively gloomy in the last few rooms.

When the lightning flashed and the thunder roared, he jumped, startled. He looked out the window of the room he was in and realized the sky had darkened to an inky black, the room wasn't gloomy because of its location or size, as he'd been thinking, but because Carol's storm had arrived with a vengeance.

The next bolt of lightning blinded him in its closeness and brilliance. The thunder that immediately followed shook the house. The wind picked up in strength and then the rain started slashing at the windows. Max knew they only had two rooms left, but decided this high up in the house probably wasn't the safest place in a lightning storm.

Carol said, "We should go down. I'm not afraid of lightning, but we're pretty far up and it's an old house."

"I was just thinking the same thing, we can wait out the storm to finish up here or come back another day."

They started down the stairs when there was the definite sound of a door slamming shut. Max frowned at the sound and felt a slight disturbance in the air. "We should check the doors."

Nodding Carol said, "Yes, but we haven't opened the back ones."

"Let's check them anyway."

They checked all three doors and found them securely closed. The rain pounded against the windows and lightning slashed the sky, the thunder emphasizing just how close they were to the center of the storm

When they got to their table in the foyer he watched as

Carol pulled out the homemade cookies and handed him one. After she'd taken a bite, she waved her cookie at him. "A door slammed, and I felt the air shift."

He nodded as he chewed the soft cookie with the gooey chocolate chips and the crunch of pecans. It was the best cookie he'd had in years, maybe ever.

"So how can all the doors be firmly closed?" The thunder seemed to underline her words.

He swallowed and glanced sadly at his nearly finished cookie. Then he looked up and met her eyes. "I have no idea. This house seems to have more mysteries than answers. We need a user's manual. I still think there should be a servant's stairs, too, but I've seen no evidence of one. It's too large of a house not to ha—" He trailed off; Carol had a distracted look on her face. Her eyes were unfocused, her face void of expression.

As the storm raged around them, he watched her, everything had turned internally for the moment. After a few minutes Max said, "Carol, what are you thinking?"

She turned toward him, her eyes focusing. "What if the poem is some kind of user's manual? Or not a user's manual but the way to find the void?"

He scoffed. "Like a treasure map?"

"No, well yes, kind of."

"It didn't make any sense."

"It didn't make any sense standing in my kitchen. But what if it did here. We've pretty much ignored everything except the dimensions of the house and rooms. But what if we really looked at the whole shebang. With the poem in our hand."

Max ran his hand down his beard and thought about her suggestion. She was right, they'd not really looked at much, like furnishings or art, or well, anything. He couldn't remember much about the poem except the first line, because it started like that well-known poem about little boy blue. But it had gone crazy right after those three words.

"It's not a bad idea." The lightning flashed and the thunder drowned out his words, but she seemed to have heard them anyway.

She took a bite of her cookie and then seemed to notice he'd eaten all of his. "Do you want another?"

"Heck yes, they are amazing."

She beamed and handed him another cookie, which he tried to eat slowly and savor, but all too soon it was gone.

She handed him one more and he felt like cheering.

"The storm is moving off," she said. "At least the lightning part of it. I don't know if we'll get daylight back in time to finish the last few rooms up there."

"That's fine, I doubt we'll find anything. Let's go back to your place and look at that poem."

CHAPTER THIRTEEN

*T*he sky was still black as ink, as they locked up the front door, and Max loaded their gear into the Outback. The rain had stopped, and the wind was almost too calm, as if it was holding its breath. The stillness was absolute. Thunder could be heard in the distance, a faint rumbling. Flashes of light appeared on the horizon. The rain had scoured the earth and left rivulets of water on the driveway.

With the inky black sky as backdrop for the building, it looked even more like a haunted house. With some of the shenanigans they had encountered he almost believed it might be haunted. Almost.

His logical mind conjured up scenario after scenario of what might have caused the door slamming sounds. Shutters banging, interior doors, even branches of the overgrown trees hitting the house. They hadn't examined the foliage when they'd done their walk around.

The keys going missing was a different story, he couldn't think of any reason why they had gotten in the lunch bag. He didn't remember seeing Carol open the bag when they'd set things down on that table. He'd been pulling out his tablet at one point and gathering up some of the supplies to take with them, so he'd not had his eyes on her the whole time, but what would be the reason for her to put them in the bag.

She certainly didn't act like she was getting senile; her mind was still sharp. She'd looked genuinely baffled, so he didn't think she'd been teasing him. Max shook his head, he honestly couldn't figure it out.

Carol was driving back to town silently, with a frown on her forehead. He could almost see her mind whirling with the same questions. He doubted she would come up with any answers other than the ones he had.

She sighed and shot him a glance. "I can't figure it out. None of it. Let's hope the poem will give us a hint."

Max didn't have a lot of confidence for that, but the worry in her gaze caused him to smile brightly, and lie to her. "Yes, there has to be some reason they included it."

Her shoulders relaxed a little at the expectation of an answer. "There must be a logical explanation. I'm not going to start believing in ghosts and haunted houses at my age."

Max chuckled at the vehemence in her voice. "I agree, but I have seen some odd things in my day. Or at least things that started out odd, usually they did resolve into natural circumstances."

"Precisely, we're at the stage where everything is odd." She nodded her head once with emphasis. "I'm sure they will all resolve when we know the facts."

"Then let's look at it like a mystery to be solved."

"I always did love a good mystery. Nancy Drew were my favorite books when I was a child."

"I enjoyed the Hardy boys as well. And still like a good mystery."

"I do too. I just finished the new JD Robb."

He groaned, "That's half mystery and half romance."

Her eyes laughed at him and he felt it down to his toes. The woman just did it for him. "Exactly, the perfect combination."

"Women," he muttered, which made her laugh.

They talked about their favorite authors and books the rest of the way to her B&B.

Carol appreciated Max turning the topic away from the house and the odd things that had happened while they were in there. She couldn't say she believed in ghosts exactly, but she had witnessed something supernatural a time or two. Nothing like keys hiding and doors slamming, but a whisper of a guiding hand from time to time.

She was certain she hadn't put the keys in with the lunch, but couldn't find another rational solution as to how they'd gotten in there. Was she losing her marbles? She honestly didn't think so, but wasn't the person losing them the last to know?

She changed out of the long-sleeved t-shirt she'd worn out to the filthy house and into a short-sleeved summer blouse. The sky was still dark from the storm and the temperature had dropped, so it might be a chilly night.

She and Max had parted ways when they got back so they could change clothes and freshen up. She'd been too anxious to shower and do her hair. She wanted to brainstorm with Max about the poem. So, she'd washed up and changed clothes. Combed out her hair and spritzed on a tiny bit of perfume. She didn't stink, but she was still a woman and Max was an attractive man.

She decided to take the whole packet down with her, just in case there was something in the letter she'd missed. Carol was going to focus on the mystery and firmly shut out any worry about those damn keys.

As she descended the stairs she thought about dinner. She didn't want pizza again. She had some of her chili, frozen in the freezer, it was a cool enough night it might taste good, even in the middle of the summer. She had salad fixings and could whip up some corn bread. Although spicy food two nights in a row might not be good. Damn, it sucked getting older, where she had to think about things like heartburn.

She thought there might also be some of her chicken noodle soup in the freezer, she could make biscuits instead of corn bread and still have a salad. The chicken noodle soup could thaw and heat while they examined the poem. Perfect.

By the time Max got down to the kitchen, she had a fresh pot of coffee on, decaf, and the chicken soup in the crockpot on high. Max was freshly showered and wore jeans and a tight navy-blue t-shirt, which fit him like skin and showed his very nice body. He was in good shape for a man his age and she appreciated the eye candy.

"I made coffee, decaf."

"Thanks, wish I could handle real this time of day, but… it sucks getting old."

"I was thinking the same thing. I thought about heating up some of my chili for dinner, but then decided that spicy food two nights in a row might not be good."

Max grimaced. "I do love a good chili, but… heartburn."

"Precisely. So, I got out my homemade chicken noodle."

He looked up with a spark of interest. "With homemade egg noodles?"

She nodded.

"Hot damn, that's one of my favorites. Even better than chili."

Happiness spread through her at his enthusiasm. "With

homemade biscuits that you can slather with homemade jam."

He groaned. "Damn woman, you're killing me."

She laughed and felt something she hadn't felt in a long time. Male appreciation for her cooking. Sure, the guests were always appreciative, but this was different. This was feeding a man, not as a guest, although he was one, but this was a dinner, together, as they worked as friends to solve a mystery. It just felt different to her and it filled her feminine heart with joy.

CHAPTER FOURTEEN

Max was looking forward to her chicken soup and biscuits. He'd already been spoiled with her breakfasts and he knew her pastries were made from scratch, but dinner felt special. He'd not had a homemade dinner in years, his wife had been a great cook and she'd often fussed on the weekends preparing something special.

But Jeanette had been gone five years. Wes and Kendra often invited him over since Jeanette's death, but Kendra was not a person who spent a lot of time in the kitchen, and there was nothing wrong with that. Women and men that had full lives didn't always have time to make things from scratch, and the food that was available these days made meal preparation easy for busy families. But he missed the homemade specialties just the same.

He thought about learning to do it himself, it just seemed like too much work for one person, and he'd never been a great cook. He could get by, but he took advantage of the offerings at the grocery store.

Before he got all mushy and sentimental, he needed to

reign it in, and the best way to do that was look at their puzzle.

Carol said, "The soup has to thaw and heat, so we can spend some time looking at the poem and eat later." She pointed to the packet on the counter. "I brought the whole packet down, in case there is something in the letter I missed."

"Do you mind if I look through it, while you finish up?"

"No, go right ahead. I'm almost done. I'll whip up the biscuits when the soup is ready."

Max pulled the contents out of the envelope. There was a deed to the house in Carol's name. A passbook from the bank in town. The poem, a fat document from the lawyer, and a letter from the previous owners.

Curiosity got the best of him and he opened the bank book. He whistled at the amount. "Well you should have no trouble renovating with that chunk of change."

"Yeah and it will probably see us into the future, too, for maintenance and utilities and even book purchases. I had no idea the Zimmermans had that kind of money stashed away. They were just normal folks."

"That's often the case. Sometimes it's the ones that look like they don't have a dime that have it squirreled away."

"Yeah, I have seen that a couple of times now."

She looked so amused he wanted to ask, but curiosity about the house overwhelmed that desire. He picked up the legal document and scanned it. Seeing nothing special in it, other than the requirement that she convert the house into a library to be used by the city.

He laid that down and picked up the letter, just as Carol joined him, bringing them both a hot cup of coffee. She'd set down a small platter of fruit and cheese to snack on while he was looking at the legal gibberish.

He put the letter down for a moment and picked up the

coffee. Taking a piece of cheese, he noticed something odd out of the corner of his eye. The letter had an odd pattern of color. He set his coffee down and popped the cheese in his mouth to pick up the letter, again.

Frowning he said, "Did you notice how some words are darker than others?"

"Yes, I did. But I just assumed it was a pen malfunctioning."

He studied the document, and the words written in a darker ink. No, he was certain it was deliberate, not a bad pen. Excitement bloomed. "I don't think so. Can you grab us some paper and a pen? I left my stuff upstairs."

Carol jumped up. "You think there's something hidden in the letter?"

"I do."

She scurried off to find paper and pen.

Carol was so darn excited. She'd seen a movie once where a message was hidden in a letter. She grabbed a spiral note-book she'd bought for when the current one she was using was filled. She kept notes on her guests, what they liked, where they visited, personal information they shared, children and grandchildren's names. When they left, she care-fully put all her notes into a database her daughter, Sandy, had made for her. That way if she had repeat customers, she had their preferences and other information at her fingertips.

Handing Max the brand-new notebook, she sat closely beside him. Carol had not paid any attention to the darker words when she'd read over the document, she'd just assumed it had been a faulty pen, but now that she looked closely, she could see they were done with a different pen entirely. One pen had a wider tip and even the ink was a slightly different color.

Max was dutifully writing down each of the darker words. She watched, but the words didn't seem to be forming sentences. Deciding to wait until he was finished, she watched his strong hands slowly and deliberately write down each word. Carol wondered if he did everything in that slow and deliberate way, and felt her body flush at the idea of those strong hands on her. Pushing that foolish thought to the side, she focused on the words again. No, they still didn't make sense. Just odd words on the page.

Max finished with the last word and sighed. "It's just gibberish."

Carol's excitement died. "That's what it looked like to me too. What if we read it backward?"

Max put his finger on the last word and moved it along. When he got to the first word on the paper, he shook his head. "Nope, still nothing that makes sense."

Carol frowned. "Maybe it's a word scramble. Write down the first letter of each word."

He dutifully did as he was told and they examined the letters and saw no pattern, there were way too many consonants.

Grasping for straws she said, "The last letter of each word?"

But no, there was nothing there either, too many words had only two letters to try anything else. She sighed. "Darn, this seems to be nothing more than an exercise in frustration. But doesn't the fact they had used two pens have to mean something?"

Max didn't answer, he just kept looking at the letter.

Defeated, Carol rose. "I'll whip up the biscuits and check the chicken, we might as well eat before we take a crack at the poem. Do you want some wine with dinner? Or I have beer."

He answered slowly, pulling his concentration from the letter. "A beer would be great, but maybe after dinner. I don't want anything to mask the flavor of your soup or jams."

Carol preened and bustled around the kitchen, while he chatted about his favorite foods. She stirred the soup and the aroma filled the kitchen. Max groaned and she assumed the scent had reached him.

"That smells delicious."

She took a tiny taste, the flavors exploded on her tongue, perfect. "It tastes delicious too."

"Hey, that's not fair." He pouted like a little boy.

"Sure, it is, the cook has to make sure it doesn't need something."

"But it was frozen so that means you tasted it when you made it originally."

"I did. Now quit whining and get whatever jam flavor you prefer out of the fridge. I think I'll have blackberry."

Max looked in the fridge and then back at her. "Are these all homemade?"

She nodded.

"Can I try more than one?"

"Sure, as many as you want."

She pulled the biscuits out of the oven and placed them in a wicker basket with a cloth napkin lining it. When she took them over to the little table, she laughed at the assortment of jams he'd picked. "I didn't know you were going to go crazy with the jam selection. I don't think I made enough biscuits for all of those."

Max shrugged. "I left two in the fridge, grape and apricot."

"What if those are my very best flavors?"

His gaze snapped to hers and she tried to hide her teasing expression.

He looked toward the fridge and then at the jars filling the table and then back at the fridge. Finally, he shook his head. "I'll just have to wait until you have those two out for the breakfast buffet. You said you didn't make enough biscuits as it is."

She laughed and went back to ladle their soup into large stoneware bowls. She sprinkled some chopped parsley on top and set the two bowls on the table. Max had gotten them both a fresh cup of coffee and glasses of water.

He rubbed his hands together and took a spoonful of her soup, careful to get chicken, noodles, and vegetables all on the spoon at the same time. Fiddling with a biscuit, she watched him, curious about his reaction. He put the bite in his mouth, moaned in appreciation and shut his eyes chewing slowly.

Carol wanted to groan herself, or maybe run away. The man made eating a spoonful of soup into an almost sexual encounter. Her nipples tightened, and warmth filled her belly, spreading lower. She sat there frozen until he opened his eyes, delight filling them.

"That is truly delicious. I haven't had soup that good in years, maybe ever. Thank you for sharing it."

She shook herself out of her stupor and spooned some of the soup into her dry mouth. It was tasty, but nothing like what Max suggested. Dear God, what was she going to do when he started tasting all those jams?

CHAPTER FIFTEEN

Max was in hog heaven, the woman knew how to cook, the chicken soup and homemade egg noodles had taken him back in time. His mother had made noodles like that and had taught his wife, knowing it was one of his favorite dishes. Carol used a few different spices, but he found it delightful just the same.

He had several more spoonfuls of soup before he could even think to try the biscuits and jam. But then he started and had a fun time trying the different jams on each bite of biscuit. The flavors were amazing. She'd put some different herbs or something in with the fruit that brought out the flavors.

He'd stopped thinking about the house and its mysteries. Too focused on trying to pick out his favorite jam and savoring the soup. Carol had refilled his bowl twice and he'd tried all the jams and was doing a final comparison between his favorite three to see if he could pick a winner.

The clatter of Carol's spoon in her bowl startled him out of his food trance. Her eyes were brimming with excitement. "What if it's the lighter words?"

Max's eyes snapped to hers. He raised an eyebrow and she leaped up to grab the notebook and the letter. Turning to a fresh page she started writing down the words in the lighter color and pen thickness. Maybe she was on to something, there had to be some reason the person had gone to all the trouble to use two pens, changing every few words.

Max gave up on his jam quest, he was getting too full anyway, and watched her write. She had a graceful hand, but her words were barely legible. He wondered if her handwriting was always that bad or if she was just excited.

When she was finished, there were a lot more words on the page. She frowned at what she'd just written. "Darn, still nothing that makes sense."

Max was across the table from her, so everything was upside down. But as he looked at the words at what was his top of the page but her bottom. He wasn't so sure of that. "Read it from the bottom up.

She shrugged and started reading. "Dear Carol, we know this is a very odd request."

She looked up at him, excitement pouring out of her gaze. "It makes sense. We did it."

The look in her eyes made her so damn sexy he was worried he might leap across the table and ravish her. He grit his teeth and ground out. "Keep reading."

Carol grinned and went back to the letter, giving him a small amount of time to get his composure together. He didn't hardly hear the next few sentences but when the letter started referencing the poem, he paid attention and scribbled on his napkin with the pen she'd laid down.

When she finished reading, she looked up at him again. This time her eyes held a storm of emotion. "This is crazy. I have to do it because the Andersons are somehow related to the Zimmermans and there is proof of that in the house.

Someone was trying to break in, so that's why all the secrets and cryptic information."

Max hadn't heard some of that, but he'd heard things she wasn't thinking about. "There were more clues in the letter. Little boy blue is on the second floor. The woman with a crown is on the first. The basement is actually the root cellar which is multiple floors and the dragon is on the lowest level. We have to find all those and take them to the library and put them in their correct places and they will show us the way."

Max shook his head. "I still don't follow all of it, but at least we know more than we did."

Carol's thoughts were whirling with all the information they had discovered. Some questions had been answered, but many more had surfaced.

"How about I make us a copy in the correct order, that is legible. Is your handwriting always that atrocious?"

She looked at the page. "Nearly, but I was excited, so it might be a little worse than normal. Are you finished with your jam competition? I'll put the food away while you make us a better copy."

Max nodded and grunted, already working on the task. Carol shook her head and moved to clean up. He did have a nice consistent writing. Block letters that seemed to be common on architectural plans. She figured he'd started as an architect back when plans were drawn, and labeled, by hand, rather than through a CAD program.

As she rinsed the plates and put the leftovers in the fridge, she thought about how much she enjoyed having a man her age in her home. She hoped he would be able to stay while she searched for the mystery in the house and help her with the renovation plans.

Maybe she should hire him as an architect to do the job fully. But Carol knew Max was not a big fan of renovations. He'd said so a couple of times. Although he did seem to be enthusiastic about the house and its secrets. Should she ask or just let him help as he wanted?

She took a small plate of cookies over to the table and refilled their coffee.

Max finished the letter and re-read it in silence, then he handed it to her, and she re-read it too. A few more things stood out to her on this reading. When she looked up, she saw Max making notes while looking at the poem. She slid the letter near him as a reference.

Max finished the note he was writing and started sharing his thoughts. "The letter and poem go in the same order even though the first item is on the second floor, the second item is on the first floor and the third item is on a subfloor. I think we need to search for them in that order. I did notice the library had one wall that was blank with no books on it. I'm guessing that might be where we line them up. I think we need to use the same order as the poem."

"I agree. I was thinking that the house is a Queen Anne, so I wonder if that has something to do with the 'Lady who is wearing a crown'."

"That's an interesting thought." He jotted it down on his list. "I wonder if the Anderson-Zimmerman connection has anything to do with it. The fact that the names run from A to Z is also interesting, don't you think?"

"It is, and it's probably something to keep in mind, as we explore the house again. Max, do you think the odd sounds we heard, and the keys being moved have anything to do with the person who had been intruding, and why the Zimmermans hid the information behind puzzles?"

Max grimaced. "I did wonder about that. We still haven't found any servant stairs."

"If there are some and an intruder found them, they could have been moving around without our knowledge."

Max looked at her with an odd light in his eyes. "You know I was so focused on the giant void, that I didn't look too closely at the rest. What I might have passed off as a closet, might be a staircase."

"It would have to be a hidden one. We were searching for doors."

"We were, but on the interior walls. Where the void is. But what if it's on an exterior wall and the door blends into the paneling or walls. Let me grab my laptop so we can see the schematic better than the little picture on my tablet."

Max hurried off and Carol sipped her coffee while she was waiting. Her gaze roving back and forth between the picture on the tablet and the papers. The last two lines of the poem mentioned treasure and damned if this wasn't feeling like a treasure hunt.

CHAPTER SIXTEEN

*M*ax was gearing up to return to the *House of Mystery* as he'd dubbed it in his mind. He and Carol had closely inspected his drawing last night and had in fact, found two possible locations for a servant's staircase. One on each side of the house. One could possibly lead off the kitchen, the other looked like it could be an exit from the house. He'd not seen a door in that location, but what if it was also concealed?

Why the people who had built the house would hide everything, he had no idea, but people were weird, and he had firsthand experience with them wanting odd things in their buildings.

He was enjoying the heck out of spending time with Carol and the mystery was intriguing, even though the church building project didn't need him anymore he was in no hurry to return home. He should probably find out if Carol wanted him to do the re-design for her, that would give him a legitimate excuse to stay longer.

Even if she didn't, he had plenty of vacation time and they weren't extremely busy at their company. Most of their work was done remotely anyway, so he could work on something new, right here in Chedwick. He could work on his laptop, he preferred his workstation with the large dual screens, but he didn't have the delightful woman or the fantastic food at home.

Yep, he was in no hurry to leave. He even wondered if he should order himself another screen that he could plug into his laptop, they weren't terribly expensive, and he could have it shipped here. That would be a great idea, if Carol wanted him to stay and be part of the project. Max firmly decided that now was the time to have that discussion.

Slinging the backpack over his shoulder he sauntered out of his room whistling *Knights in White Satin*. Why the Moody Blues song had popped into his head he had no idea. He'd been a little kid when it had hit the top of the charts. His mom had loved it, so he'd heard it plenty of times, but it was still odd.

Max shrugged and headed toward the stairs. Carol was just setting the food by the door, for him to carry out to her SUV, when he walked into the kitchen, seems they'd gotten themselves into a routine. Maybe that should freak him out, but it didn't.

Carol asked, her eyes flashing in enthusiasm, "Are you ready for our treasure hunt?"

"I am indeed, and you?"

"Raring to go."

She took the keys and the cooler of drinks and they went out to the car. After the discovery of the person who had been intruding, Max had gone out this morning, while Carol tended to her guests, and bought a nice new padlock and chain for the gates. They'd decided to start keeping the place more secure. They didn't know if there was a person sniffing around for certain, but it seemed likely. A person was much more believable than a ghost.

Carol said, "Since it rained yesterday, do you think we should look around for footprints outside that aren't ours?"

Max pondered that. It might make sense, but he hated the idea of wasting the precious daylight hours outside rather than exploring for the items mentioned in the poem. "That's not a bad idea, but I think it would be best to concentrate on our treasure hunt inside for now. If we find what we're looking for we can worry about an intruder later."

"Oh goody, I was hoping you would pick that, but I felt obligated to bring it up."

He wondered if he was being foolish to not concentrate on a possible threat, so he said, "If we find any evidence of someone in the house, besides ourselves, it might be a good idea to get the police involved."

Carol tapped a finger to her lips. "Not a bad idea. Our police chief is a pretty mellow guy, but he's on vacation right now, berry picking in Chelan, he'll be back in a few days. I would want to have him be the one we talk to. Do you think it would hurt to wait a few days?"

"No, not really. I think we'll be fine." Max hoped what he'd just said was the truth.

Carol's grip on the steering wheel relaxed, she was a little more concerned than she was letting on. "So, should we look for the servant's staircase first or go with the poem?"

"Since we have a general vicinity for a staircase or two, let's start with those two areas and then we can move to the poem. Besides if we find the staircase, we might find intruder evidence."

Carol tensed back up, just a little. He wouldn't have noticed it if he hadn't been paying close attention to her body language. "Sounds like a plan."

He decided that maybe the quest to discover if there was someone lurking around might be more important than the treasure hunt. At least to soothe Carol's nerves.

~

Max opened the gates and Carol drove through them, he shut the gates behind them. They'd talked about putting the lock on the gates while they were inside the house, but for some reason, that idea didn't sit well with either of them. So, he pulled the gates shut but didn't lock them.

Carol had already decided she was going to talk to Nolan about a security system for the house, at the very least motion sensors for the front gate. Although no one had walked the grounds, so it was entirely possible that the front gate was not the only entrance, whether by design or because time had allowed the fence to run to disrepair.

There was so much to do. She already had a list in her head and wasn't quite sure where to start. Cleaning would be a big priority, the ground maintenance another, then the electricity needed inspection, and finally reconstruction. She was excited about the whole idea, but also a little over-whelmed. Fortunately, this had waited to rear its ugly, but exciting, head, until after her B&B was running well and not taking all of her time anymore.

Carol could always go to the mayor to talk through her issues, he had been the chief of police before she'd practically forced him to become mayor. But she wasn't quite ready to bring the city into the idea, yet. She wanted a good plan before she started that ball rolling. She wasn't one to go off halfcocked.

No, she would wait until Nolan got back and she could run her concerns by him. He'd not lived here all his life and kept a secret better than some of the others might.

When they got into the house they went straight to the kitchen and pulled up the detailed drawing of the area where they thought the staircase might be. They examined the wall where lots of hooks hung. Carol could imagine all kinds of

86

pots and pans and utensils hanging from those hooks. She couldn't decide if it was an efficient use of the space or a waste. Most people hung pans and utensils above the work-space, rather than taking up a whole wall.

She mentioned the thought to Max, but he just shrugged and kept looking for some kind of opening. Carol was intrigued however and continued to study the wall, she noticed one hook that was different from the rest. It was larger and probably used to hold something big and heavy like a cast iron pot of some kind. The rest of the hooks were to the left of the big one, it seemed to be all alone. It was long and square. She ran a finger over it wondering about its purpose.

It was slightly crooked, so she went to straighten it. And it moved easily all the way to the right and she heard a clicking sound. A slight movement of the wall, suggested it might open further. Excitement surged.

"Um, Max?"

"Yeah?" he said not looking away from where he was studying the wall in a pantry.

"I think I found it."

"What did you find?"

"The door. But it's kind of stuck."

His head snapped around and his eyes lit with excite-ment. Max came over and looked at what she'd done. "Looks like it might be on a track, like a pocket door. I'll get the WD-40. Good job!"

Max hesitated and looked at her for a long moment. She held her breath, for one heartbeat she thought he might hug her or even kiss her, but instead he gave her a high five, like they were frat buddies. She wanted to punch him, she wasn't a damn frat buddy, she was a woman. But then she decided it was best that they kept this all on a friend level. Darn it.

It took them a few minutes and some muscle to get the

door open. Max used the WD-40 liberally but the door hadn't opened enough for them to get to even a portion of the track. They set their flashlights down and Max even took off his backpack when it kept bumping into her. It took both of them to wedge the door open enough for Max to use more of the lubricant.

When they resumed pushing and pulling on the door it still wasn't moving except for a tiny bit. She pushed and he pulled, over and over again, each tiny bit of movement he applied more of the oil. They got it open enough for them to finally get a tiny bit of leverage, with one mighty yank the door slid open and they both tumbled inside the empty space. Once their hands were off the door it slid smoothly shut and they were encased in darkness.

The space was tiny, and the darkness was complete.

Max muttered, "Damn, should have wedged something in the door."

Carol nodded and hit her head on his chin, they were cramped together body to body in the suffocating space.

Max huffed out a breath. "You, Carol Anderson, have a hard head. Can you find a door handle on the inside?"

She turned her back to him and felt around. But didn't even know where to search. The wood on the inside was rough and as she searched, she felt a sliver get caught in one finger.

"Oww, I got a sliver."

"Darn, sorry. Can we trade places, so I can search?"

They managed to trade places with a lot of bodily contact which was causing trouble of a different kind. While he searched, she tried to ignore the proximity of the hot man. She felt the stairs rise up at her back and stepped up on the first one, but the complete darkness gave her vertigo, so she stepped back down to the floor.

Unknown to her, Max had turned toward her when she'd

moved away, when she stepped back down, they were in full body contact from knees to chest. The bump between them caused both of them to almost lose their balance, but they both reached out and caught the other one. Her hands on his arms, his hands on her hips.

His voice was gruff when he asked, "Are you all right?"

She nodded and bumped his chin again. He let out a little huff of breath at the contact. "Are you trying to kill me?"

She laughed and tilted her face up to him, keeping her head back from his chin. "No, but I seem to be succeeding. My head likes your chin, I guess."

They stilled in the darkness and the air grew heavy between them. "Carol?"

"Yeah?"

"I want to kiss you."

"Do you think that's a good idea?"

"No, not at all, but here we are, trapped in the dark, and…"

She huffed out a breath, understanding completely how he was feeling. Her voice was low and sounded needy to her own ears. "Just one small one, just to get it out of our system."

His mouth descended and even though they couldn't see a thing, he had perfect aim.

They kissed for long moments, first soft and gentle, and then growing in strength and intimacy. He tasted like mint toothpaste and man. His mouth was firm and his tongue, when she opened her mouth to admit him, was coaxing and probing. Sparks shot through her body as he claimed her with his mouth. His hands never moved an inch, even though her thoughts willed them to.

When they finally broke for air, she felt his gaze rise above her head. "I see a tiny glint of light."

"What? Where?"

"Up the stairs, I guess my eyes finally adjusted." He turned back toward the door. "Not enough to see down here, but there must be another door up higher, maybe we can get out there."

She looked up the stairs and could also see the tiny glow. "But without the lubricant will it open?"

"This door is near the kitchen and a lot of steam, up higher we might not need it. Let me go first."

They shuffled around again, and Carol clearly felt Max's erection, but she didn't mention it. He probably felt her hard as rock nipples, too. Their scents had gotten stronger from the kiss also and she was nearly dizzy from the, oh so appealing, smell of aroused male. But she tamped it down, they needed to get out of the staircase.

CHAPTER SEVENTEEN

hen they emerged from the stairs Max let out a breath he'd been holding. The light he'd seen was a tiny window on the second level, which gave them enough light to find the door. It opened easily compared to the kitchen entrance and led into a sitting room.

Carol followed him out and she also let out a huge breath and then looked at her finger. He remembered the splinter and bent his head to look. "Let me see it. I have a small first aid kit with tweezers in my back pack."

She let him examine it, it didn't look too bad, but tweezers would help. Part of it was sticking out so he didn't think it would take but a minute to get it out and put some antibiotic cream on it.

Carol gasped and he looked up, had he hurt her? Her eyes were staring across the room. He followed her gaze, but all he saw was dusty walls and an even dustier picture.

"We should go down to the kitchen and get my backpack and fix up your finger."

"The finger can wait. Look."

He turned to look where she was pointing at the dusty picture on the wall. He frowned, what was so interesting about a dusty picture… of little boy blue. Their first clue was right there directly across from the opening to the staircase.

Max turned back to her and grinned. "Good job, I never would have noticed."

She grinned back at him and they walked over to the picture. He pulled the picture away from the wall and saw it was hanging by a simple hook and lifted it carefully off the wall.

Carol gasped again. "There's a tiny door."

He set the painting down on the floor leaning it against the wall. Sure enough, there was a tiny door in the wall behind where the picture hung. He pulled it open and peered inside, wishing he had his flashlight. There didn't seems to be anything inside though, except for a little sliver of metal. He pulled it out and held it up to the light, but couldn't begin to determine what it might be for.

"Any ideas?"

Carol shook her head. "None whatsoever, but bring it with you. We can take these things down to the library."

"After we doctor your finger and get our stuff out of the kitchen."

"My finger is fine."

"I'm sure it is, but we're going to doctor it just the same. We don't want you getting an infection when you don't need to. And I am going to put my mini flashlight into my pocket, just in case of any more darkness incidents."

Carol flushed a very pretty color and he wondered if she was thinking more about the kiss than being trapped in the dark.

It only took a moment to get the splinter out of her finger, but the feel of her soft skin in his hand put him on edge, they definitely had some kind of connection he'd never encountered before. He'd not felt it with his wife, but they'd grown up together and had been friends in grade school. Their friendship had morphed into love, a love so powerful they never wanted to be apart. Which was why he wasn't dealing with her death well. It felt like a piece of him was gone, and it wasn't a little piece, no it was a huge chunk that just wasn't there anymore.

So, this infatuation he was feeling for Carol was completely new and he didn't quite know what to do with it.

Carol was feeling a bit overwhelmed by Max's presence. After that kiss in the dark, her body seemed highly charged and too aware of his every move. She'd about combusted while he pulled the splinter out, applied the antibiotic ointment, and bandaged it. It had seemed like it was taking forever as her body and mind reacted to his attentions, but she knew it had been just a few short moments.

Finally, he had moved away, and she could breathe again. Then they had taken their first clue to the library. They wanted to find the other two before they did anything with it, so they leaned it up against the wall.

"Let's go see if we can find the second staircase. We probably want to go back into the one we were in and explore it with our flashlights but let's do that later."

Carol was all onboard with that idea, she wasn't ready to visit the scene of the kiss so soon. "Great idea," she said a little too enthusiastically.

Max just nodded and led the way to the room they suspected had the door to another staircase. Now that they knew what they were looking for, it only took a few minutes to find the door which then opened easily. A little too easily.

Max pushed it open and in the bright room saw the latch

to keep it open. "Don't go in yet. This doesn't seem quite right."

He knelt down and ran his finger along the track. Max said, "Oil, just as I suspected, this door has been used recently."

Carol shown her flashlight into the staircase landing, it was quite a bit larger than the one they'd been trapped in. "There are footprints in the dust too. There are too many of them to gauge the size. Someone's been in there more than once."

He wiped his oily finger on his jeans and stood. "You're right, and I think that on the other side is an exit to the outside. I don't think there's any reason we can't add to the footprints in the landing. I think maybe we should avoid the stairs where there might be some better evidence for the police."

She nodded, "All right, I am dying of curiosity."

Max turned on his flashlight and led the way. On the outside wall was a door with a normal handle. "I probably shouldn't touch it in case there are fingerprints, but I'm going to anyway."

Before she could stop him, he opened the door which swung open, quietly, on well-oiled hinges.

He stepped outside and examined the door. "Ah, now I see it. There is a slightly indented brick with a veneer over part of it for a handle. Clever."

Max took a step back and lost his grip on the door and it slammed shut. Carol now knew where the door banging sounds had come from. This outside entryway swung shut quickly and echoed loudly. It only took Max a second to reappear.

"I think we found the ghost."

"Yeah. Is there any way to lock the door?"

He stepped back inside. "Let's look. Maybe we can make the ghost use the front door."

Carol giggled. It was a ridiculous sound for a woman her age, but it bubbled out before she could stop it.

"Found it. Let's go back out into the room."

Carol turned and did as he suggested. This time there was no convenient painting waiting for them to find.

"Let's have lunch, we need to decide a few things. Are you hungry?"

"I could eat."

They got the food out and settled in. Carol asked, "So, what did you want to talk about?"

Max swallowed the bite of chicken wrap and said, "I'm not sure how much more we should continue to explore before the police get out here and investigate. We could corrupt evidence they might need. I really shouldn't have opened that exterior door. The only person who had touched it in a couple of decades was the intruder."

She knew that was true, but she was also glad he had investigated enough to lock the door for the future. "You're probably right about that. But other than the staircase in the kitchen and the one picture, we haven't touched a lot more."

He gave her an odd look. "Just all the doorknobs in the whole house."

She'd forgotten all about those. Darn they might have mucked up all the evidence. Even tramping around the whole house inside and out their first day. "Oh, yeah, oops. But that was before we knew there was an intruder or even the possibility of there being one. We didn't know there was some kind of treasure. I suppose we might have guessed from the poem, but we just thought that was nonsense."

"I agree we didn't know better then, but we do now. So, I propose we lock it up tight until your chief of police gets back and then we let him investigate before we return and look for the other two clues."

Well damn, did he have to go being all rational? She didn't want to stop. She sighed. "I suppose you're right. What shall we do in the meantime? Oh! I didn't mean to insinuate you, um…"

He laughed. "No, now don't get all flustered. That was the second thing I wanted to ask you about. I'm enjoying this mystery and this house. Would you like to work with me on some renovation ideas? I'd be happy to sketch you up some suggestions. Or if you want, we can make this a formal arrangement."

"A formal arrangement?" What was he talking about? Was he some kind of a sleuth on the side? Or was this idea about their shared kiss?

"Yes, you hire me as your architect for remodeling."

Idiot. She relaxed and let out a nervous chuckle. "Oh, of course. I think that's a good idea."

"Great. Let's make sure the rest of the doors are securely locked and we'll put the chain and padlock on the gates. Do you think we should take the Little Boy Blue painting with us?"

"That might be a good idea, that way if the other person gets in, they will be missing a key part of the puzzle."

Max said, "I probably should check in with the church to see if they need anything. I don't think they will, but it doesn't hurt to drop by."

Carol nodded. "It's probably good for me, too, that we're laying off the investigation for a few days. I have some new people coming in, so it would probably be good to stick around my house until Nolan and Kristen get back from Chelan. I think I'll give him a call for a heads up and find out when they will be back."

"Sounds like we have a plan."

They finished lunch, checked the doors and windows on the first floor, carted all their stuff including the picture out to the car, locked the gates with the new lock, and headed for the B&B.

CHAPTER EIGHTEEN

Max walked along the sidewalk on the way to the church, he was going to spend the morning there checking on the construction and making sure they didn't need anything from him. It was a beautiful spring morning without a cloud in the sky. It was early enough that the temperature was still cool, later in the day it would warm up, but this morning it was perfect.

Working with Carol this afternoon was something he was looking forward to, when they could get started mapping out renovations for the first floor to create a library. He had some ideas and a laundry list of what a library would need, she probably had some ideas as well. He would have to determine which were the weight-bearing walls and which were not.

Aside from the house modifications, he was also spending a lot of time thinking about the kiss that he and Carol had indulged in. It had been sizzling. He hadn't mentioned it and neither had she. But just because they hadn't talked about it didn't make it any less real. He didn't know if, or what, he should do about it. Maybe they should at least talk about it, and decide how they wanted to handle it, and even more importantly, decide if they intended to pretend it never happened and never do it again, or if they would like to explore.

He pondered all these things as he walked briskly down the street toward the church. It really was a most exceptionally beautiful day and Max had a spring in his step and a lightness in his heart, that he couldn't deny.

About a block before he got to the church his cell rang, it was his brother, so he answered it.

"Good morning, Wes. How's it going?" he said cheerfully.

Wes paused for a moment and then said, "I was calling to ask you that same question. Are you doing okay today? I didn't hear from you yesterday, so I thought I would check in."

Max frowned, not quite sure what his twin was alluding to, and then it hit him so hard he felt like a freight train rolled over him. Yesterday was the sixth anniversary of his wife's death. It was like a punch to his solar plexus as the air whooshed from his lungs.

How in the hell had he forgotten? And had he really been kissing Carol Anderson on the very day, nearly the same hour he'd lost his beloved wife? What kind of an ass was he?

He said gruffly, "I'm doing all right. I've been busy helping at the old mansion, so it's kept me busy. There is a bit of a mystery going on and we found evidence of someone sneaking around in there."

Wes let out a sigh. "That's great, I'm glad you're keeping busy enough not to spiral into your normal depression."

Max didn't necessarily agree with that; shouldn't he honor his wife somehow on the day of her death and feel bad she wasn't with him? But no, he'd been with another woman and had even kissed her. He was a total asshole.

"Thanks Brother, anything new at the office?"

"A small renovation job came in, so I'm working on that. They'll be breaking ground soon on the apartments, one of us could go to that if we want but it's a multi-year project so no real need to be on hand."

"I'm on my way to the church to see if they need anything more. I doubt they will, but it doesn't hurt to check. Carol wants me to draw up some ideas for renovating the old house into a library, so I'll be sticking around for a while to work on that, and also help with the mystery."

"What is the mystery?"

"There is a void in the center of the house that indicates a hidden room of some sort. "

"Well, that *is* interesting."

"Yeah and there is a letter with some cryptic clues. So once the police chief gathers any intruder evidence, we'll be following those clues to see where they lead."

"Your own version of clue."

Max chuckled. "Well I hope no one has died, but yes, it is a mystery."

"Good, I hope it keeps your mind occupied. Maybe you can finally start healing."

Max didn't want to get into it with his brother, grief was not the same for everyone and he knew his brother didn't understand, and he hoped his brother didn't understand for many years to come.

He grunted out a response to that statement and then said, "I'm almost to the church, so I'll let you go and talk to you later."

"Sounds good, call if you need to. I'm always here for you."

"I will, talk to you later. Thanks for calling." Max didn't know if he was glad his brother had called or not. After he hung up, he stepped into the current church building for a bit of quiet, before he went to the building site. He slipped into the back of the sanctuary and saw a very pregnant Nicole, the pastor's wife, on the drums. She was pounding out a primal rhythm that he felt throughout his whole body. As he sat in the back with the drums reverberating through his being, he thought about his wife and how he missed her, but also how he'd let the day of her death slip past him. On one hand he was horrified he'd forgotten about it, and on the other, he was glad he hadn't started the spiral into the depression, that normally hit him.

Carol danced through her chores at the B&B. She got the rooms turned for the people coming in. She prepped some breakfast dishes for tomorrow and planned out her menus for next week. Once the planning was done, she looked at her supplies and put in an order for Safeway to deliver to the ferry tomorrow.

But no matter how much she tried to keep herself busy, the kiss in the dark she'd shared with Max kept popping up. Every time it crept into her consciousness her body reacted to the memory. Bad body. But she couldn't blame it. The kiss had been extraordinary. The man certainly knew how to kiss. She'd been on fire when they had finally pulled apart to catch their breath.

She wondered if she should say something about it to Max. The real question was *what* did she want to say? No more of that. It was just a fluke. Let's pretend it didn't happen. Or. Can we do it again? And again? Do we want to investigate the attraction further?

Her thoughts kept going around and around in circles. Listing off all the reasons the kiss was a bad idea, then all the reasons it was a good thing. She was practically dizzy from all the introspection.

Carol needed to stop this craziness right now. This was ridiculous. She had another hour or two before Max would be back, so they could work on the renovation plans, she decided to bake, bread, from scratch. Maybe mini-loaves that she could warm up and set out for breakfast.

Max walked in just as she put the last pan of bread into the oven to bake, this was the third batch of eight mini-loaves. "Are you ready?" he asked in a clipped manner.

She looked up feeling startled by his tone, he'd always been laid back and friendly, but this time his voice was professional and definitely cool. Not at all what she had been expecting. But she would take his lead. She shut the oven and started the timer. "Yes. "I'll need to pull those out when they are done baking, but that's all. Do you mind working here in the kitchen?"

He looked over at the kitchen table in the breakfast nook, frowned, then nodded. "I'll go get my laptop."

She watched him go and wondered what was wrong. He'd seemed fine this morning at breakfast, she hoped it wasn't something at the church.

When he'd put everything on the table and moved into the enclosed space, leaving her room to sit on the end she asked, "Would you like something to drink?"

Max started to shake his head and then said, "Yes, a glass of tea would be nice."

She poured them both a glass and took them over to the table. He stiffened when she scooted into the booth. "Is something wrong? Is there a problem at the church?"

"No, the building is going well there."

He didn't say anything else just clicked around with the cordless mouse.

Carol sat there in an awkward silence. She'd never felt this tension from Max before. Even when she was feeling skittish around him, it hadn't been as tension-filled as today was.

Max pointed to the screen. "I think I've identified the weight bearing walls. These walls I've highlighted run through each story of the house. There may be others on the main floor, but I think we can be fairly certain these need to stay put."

He'd said that with a distant air, like he would speak to a client or total stranger, not someone whom he'd had his tongue down their throat. "All right."

He then listed some of the rooms he thought they should have, in the same clipped tone.

She didn't want to spend the afternoon with this cranky know it all. "Max, what's wrong?"

"Nothing. I'm just giving you my professional advice."

"Yes. I can hear that. Mr. Radcliff, what happened to the Max I've been spending every day with?"

He sighed. "I just thought we should proceed on a more professional level."

"Why, because you kissed me?"

He flinched. "It was inappropriate."

"Maybe, but you weren't acting this way at breakfast. What changed?"

He ran a hand over his head and down to his beard where he tugged on it. "If you must know my brother called me this morning to make sure I was doing okay. Yesterday was the anniversary of my wife's death and I usually celebrate it by getting drunk and depressed."

"Ah, but yesterday you spent it investigating a mystery, kissing me, and eating some of Hank's prime steaks cooked on the barbecue. Are you feeling guilty about that?"

"No... maybe...yes. Yes, I should have remembered and honored her."

Carol sighed. "So, you're beating yourself up, because you

weren't properly mourning her, but were on an adventure with me, that included a kiss. What would your wife think about that?"

Max's gaze drilled into hers for a long moment and she could see him looking inward for a long time, then he chuckled. "She would probably hug you for finally getting through to me, and tell me to get over myself, that it was time to move on."

"In that case, you need to do what she would have said… if she had the chance."

CHAPTER NINETEEN

*M*ax relaxed and settled in, he let what Carol had said float in the back of his mind, while they started earnestly working on ideas to convert the old mansion into a library.

"You'll only want one door for people to use, so that everyone enters and leaves through the same place. The foyer would work for that, you could have check-out stands and a book return and a librarian or two for questions. Since the books won't all be in one room, you'll need a map to show people where to go, and flyers with that same information."

"What will we do with the other doors? Not the secret one, but the other two?"

"I was thinking the one in the back that opens into the parlor could be a processing room. Books could be delivered through that door and then they could get their library bar-code and whatever else is needed, heavy plastic to protect the covers or something."

"That makes sense, although we're a pretty small town, so I don't envision lots of deliveries."

"While that may be true, it's still better to get deliveries in a location that's not in public view. You don't want to be mugged for the new Nora Roberts or James Patterson book before you can get the bar code on."

Carol laughed. "I see your point."

Her laugh skittered through him and he lost his train of thought. What in the hell were they talking about, all he could think about was that laugh and how he could get her to do it more often? Or what other sounds coming from her would do to his body, like a moan or a gasp as he did sexy things to her? Whoa, he needed to reign these thoughts in and get his brain back on renovations before there was no blood left in his head. He looked at his computer, to see if it offered a clue as to what he had been talking about. Oh yes, the other doors. "The kitchen, and the door there, I thought that area could be made into an employee break room."

"Good idea. We could put in a microwave, a refrigerator, and coffee machine. Shelves to hold personal belongings and a coat rack. Not a lot of work would be needed other than getting rid of the appliances in there and cleaning the place up."

Max tapped the table. "The plumbing and electricity might both need upgrading, but those two things will need to be checked over the whole house. Anyway, that takes care of the doors."

"I wish we knew what was in the void. If it's one big room or a bunch of tiny ones. It could be the family mausoleum for all we know," Carol said.

"Or a giant treasure room."

"Or a bunch of bedrooms."

He chuckled, "Or a storage room for old furniture and crap."

"Maybe it's a ballroom."

"Or a man cave."

"Ha! Maybe it's a man cave on the first floor, a she shed on the second, a playroom on the third, and a... an aviary on the forth."

Max barked out a shout of laughter and Carol joined him as mirth surrounded them. Their eyes met, sharing the hilarity of their ideas, laughter making her eyes sparkle and her skin glow in happiness. Suddenly the atmosphere changed, and their shared gazes morphed from laughter to something hotter, something dangerous. He wanted to capture her head in his hands and her mouth with his own. He wanted to drink her in. Heat flared in her eyes and he leaned toward her, ready to taste those sweet lips again, when the back door banged open.

They jerked back just as her son Terry charged in the room.

Carol looked at her son, and couldn't decide if she was glad he'd barged in when he did, or whether she wanted to throttle him. She'd almost kissed Max again, or he had almost kissed her, actually they'd almost kissed each other, they'd both been on the move, their lips acting like magnets, drawing them closer and closer. Damn.

"Mom," Terry said skidding to a halt. "Oh, sorry I didn't know you were busy. Hi Max, how's the building at the church going?"

"Good, actually. I'm not doing much with that anymore. We think we have all the details locked down."

"Good. So, will you be leaving soon?"

"Not too soon. I'm helping your mother with the feasibility of renovating the Zimmerman house."

Terry chuffed out a derisive sound. "That's a fool's errand if you ask me. It's been abandoned for years."

Max shook his head. "On the contrary the building is remarkably sound. We've found no water damage or creature infestation of any kind, other than a few spiders."

"Even so, Mom has enough on her plate with the B&B and—"

Carol interrupted her son, she'd already heard his opinion. "We're just trying to decide if it's viable or not. What did you want?"

Terry shuffled his feet for a moment, looking sheepish and she wondered what was going on. Then he straightened and blurted out, "I came to see when Deborah, the photographer, was coming back. I've been working on a blanket chest for her and want to make sure I have it ready for her in time."

Carol raised her eyebrows, she'd seen Terry's project planning and didn't believe what he'd said for one minute. His project planning spanned four full-sized white boards and were so in depth a person needed to be an engineer to read them. She decided not to call him on the obvious falsehood in front of Max.

"She'll be here in mid-August, she's coming then to see if she can get both late summer and early fall pictures. She's planning to stay about a month this time, to catch the leaves turning."

Terry groaned. "A month? Good grief. Well I gotta get going. Thanks, Mom. See ya, Max." He left the house muttering something that had to do with Siberia.

Max and Carol exchanged amused glances, and without mentioning the almost kiss, went back to the renovation ideas. Terry had broken the mood, and again Carol wasn't completely sure whether she was relieved by that or not.

CHAPTER TWENTY

Two days later the police chief, Nolan Thompson, and his family, got back from their trip to Chelan. Max was itching to get back inside the house, so he offered to go with Carol to talk to Nolan and let him do his investigation.

While they'd waited for Nolan to get back to town, he and Carol had spent the afternoons working on renovation ideas. They'd managed to keep their interactions on a friendly and professional level. No more heated gazes or almost kisses. Max knew it was for the better, but he'd also felt vaguely disappointed.

Max shook his head at his own foolishness and went down to meet Carol.

Nolan was waiting outside the gate when they arrived.

While Carol talked with Nolan, Max unlocked the gates and pulled them open.

Nolan had acquiesced to Carol's request to meet with her without other members on the force. At least for the initial meeting.

He heard Carol thank Nolan for coming alone.

He couldn't quite hear what Nolan said in response, but it must have been a question as to why she'd asked for that.

"I just don't want to get the whole town in an uproar until we can determine if the idea is feasible. Our small town would be alit with gossip before we even got the door unlocked."

Nolan chuckled, "True enough. News does travel fast." His eyes slid to Max. "Wes, welcome ba— You're not Wes."

Max laughed and held out his hand. "Very astute, Chief. I'm Max Radcliff, Wes's twin brother. Nice to meet you."

"Nice to meet you, too. I guess I was too wrapped up in vacation plans to hear about you through the grapevine."

Carol grinned. "I remember those days well. Trying to get two, or in my case, three little kids and all their stuff ready for a week-long vacation, took at least two weeks on the front end and three weeks on the back."

Nolan sent her a sly look. "Which is why I wasn't the least bit sad to hear from you about this project. It got me off the hook for a couple of hours."

Carol nodded slowly. "And then you'll need to meet with your staff to see what you missed. Talk to the one you left in charge and you could schedule a meeting with the mayor."

Nolan laughed. "I could, but then when I got home Kristen would shoot me dead and bury me in the backyard. Or fire up the kiln and slowly feed me into it."

Max shuddered at the thought, for some reason that sounded especially gruesome. He cleared his throat. "I think we should get a move on then, so this Kristen person doesn't get any ideas."

Nolan grinned. "My wife, and we've got a couple of hours since she was headed out to check in at the art gallery. We lined up a babysitter, before we ever left town, who can watch the kids during their naptime. It was a pre-requisite for the trip."

Carol said, "Well whichever one of you thought of that is brilliant. The kids are always cranky and exhausted after a trip like that, and need a good long nap in their own beds."

As they walked up to the house and unlocked the door, they filled Nolan in on all their doings in the house, so far.

Nolan faced them in the foyer, hands on his hips. "So, you found positive proof someone has been in the house, uninvited, and then you proceeded to muck up the evidence trail? Are you both serious right now? For crying out loud, it's not like you're teenagers and don't know any better. I don't see any signs of dementia in either of you. You couldn't wait two days until I got back?"

Carol shrugged. "We did lock the door so the intruder couldn't get back in."

"Provided you hadn't just locked him in the house." Frustration was pouring off Nolan in waves.

Max couldn't sit back and let Carol take the blame. "It was my fault. I wanted to see how they had disguised the door from the outside. Plus, we'd been searching in the house for two days before we began to suspect someone else was in here. It wasn't until we deciphered the letter that we began to put two and two together."

Nolan looked from him to Carol and back and then relaxed. "All right. The damage is done, let's see what else we might find. Besides, maybe you did lock him out rather than in. Let's start with the secret passage, there might still be some evidence left."

Carol breathed a sigh of relief when Nolan left them. It had been a tense afternoon. "Thank God, he found some evidence. I was afraid he might strangle us if he wasn't able to find any."

"He does seem a little intense."

"Nolan is very dedicated and serious about the law."

"That, my dear, is an incredible understatement. The guy is borderline fanatic."

She nodded. "Which is why we have a very safe town. No one gets away with anything. He'd arrest his own mother if she did something wrong."

Max looked out the window. "We've still got a couple of hours of daylight. Want to search the first floor for the lady who is wearing a crown?"

"Might as well, we're here."

They searched every room on the main floor and found nothing. No pictures of any females. No crown shapes of any kind. They'd even examined the carpet and the wallpaper and found nothing.

Carol frowned in frustration. "I didn't think it would be this hard. Why was the first one so easy? Come out of the secret passage, look directly in front of you and voila there it was, right in front of our faces."

"Maybe each clue gets harder." Max ventured cautiously, he obviously knew when a woman was venting and didn't want to get in the way of that.

She chuckled. "Okay, no need to hide. I was just hoping it would slap us in the face like the first one. We look up and there it is, in the most obvious place of all, but here, we come in the door and the only picture in the whole room is one of the house."

They both stilled and turned toward each other. "A picture of the house," he said.

"A Queen Anne Victorian house."

They both turned slowly and looked at the picture. Sure enough, the house looked like it was wearing a crown. A crown of sunshine, dirty sunshine, dulling the bright rays of sunlight that shot upward.

She leapt at him with enthusiasm. "We found it."

He caught her waist and twirled her around in a circle. "We did."

She laughed in pure joy and noticed a change in his eyes. An awareness that hadn't been there before. He slowly slid her to the ground and held her steady until her feet were under her, her body was nearly plastered to his, from knees to chest. Every molecule in her being reacted to that closeness with a vengeance.

Carol moved closer and his arms came around her, almost an automatic reaction. She wanted more. She leaned in and pressed a kiss to his throat.

He groaned and pulled her even closer. She lifted her face from his neck—looking up to him—offering her lips. Max didn't hesitate to take what she offered. His mouth descended to hers and gently caressed her lips. Lightning flooded her body at that gentle touch of his.

She wanted more.

Carol opened her mouth and nipped at his bottom lip to make sure he was aware of her, and her actions. His tongue swept into her mouth to duel with hers. His hands moved from her waist to her ass, where he squeezed and drew her in closer. She could feel his erection through four layers of clothing, as if there was nothing between them.

"Max," she moaned out.

He swallowed and ground out, "Carol."

She could barely tell what he was saying, his voice so low and raspy. She thrilled at the sound and the feel of his erection pushing at the zipper of his pants.

He lifted her so she could wrap her legs around his waist, his mouth devouring hers in the process. Her bad hip restricted her movements with a sharp stab of pain, but then it faded when she forced her legs to comply to her wishes.

But he must have felt her wince, because he stopped the sensual onslaught of her mouth and looked up.

"What's wrong?"

"Nothing."

"I felt you wince in pain. Is it your hip?"

Carol sighed, darn it, she didn't want to talk. She wanted to be swept away by lust and by a hard, aroused man. If they stopped to talk, they would shatter the mood and go back to being friends and co-sleuths. She tried to ignore the question by nibbling on his neck.

Max was not distracted by her antics and said, "No more until you tell me the truth."

"No, if we stop to talk, we'll stop all together and go back to being strangers on a mission. I want to be swept away by lust."

He chuckled. "We don't have to stop."

"Good, then proceed."

He chuckled again. "We don't have to stop permanently, but I don't want to hurt you. So, we could stop temporarily just until we can get back to a soft surface. And maybe also hunt up some protection."

"I have protection at home. I should have brought it with me. I just didn't think…"

"You didn't think some guy from the city was going to hit on you and put your suggestions to use?" he asked with one brow lifted in mockery.

Carol huffed and let her legs drop from around his waist. Clearly lust had lost the battle to words. Dammit.

"Well since you're too busy talking to make me scream in pleasure, we might as well lock this place up." She turned out of his arms to look up at the painting. "Should we take the pict—eep."

He took her arm and whirled her back, lifting her up by her elbows until she was on her tiptoes. His mouth descended on hers in a hot open-mouthed kiss that fired her blood back to boiling. When they needed to breathe, he broke the kiss and ground out, "I plan to make you scream with an orgasm, Carol, not with pain in your hip."

She looked into his eyes and read the truth along with the promise and smiled a slow seductress smile. "Well, then let's get back to the inn where there are lots of beds and protection."

"Just how old is that protection?"

"Brand new, I just bought it."

"For me?"

"Yes, of course, for you. Now let's quit dawdling and get out of here."

He moved so fast he was a blur, gathering up their supplies and pulling her out of the house. He loaded the car while she locked the door. He was equally efficient with the lock on the gates. The man could really move when he was properly motivated. She hoped she could remember how it all worked.

CHAPTER TWENTY-ONE

The tension was high in the car as she drove back to her house. She wanted to be carefree and happy about breaking her long sexual fast, but she was nervous. It had been a long time since a man had seen her naked. Her stomach had a pouch from carrying three kids, her breasts sagged, and her ass did too. There were wrinkles, scars, dry skin, and God only knew what else.

She pulled into the parking area and sighed. "Maybe this isn't such a great idea."

"Why not?" Max asked with a typical male attitude.

She didn't want to go into all her physical flaws. "What if I don't remember how it works?"

Max chuckled. "Pretty simple, tab A goes into slot B."

"Max!" she huffed out in surprise, tinged with a little embarrassment.

"Well it's true. You have three kids so you must have known at some time. It's kind of like riding a bike." He waggled his eyebrows. "I would be happy to instruct you."

Carol felt her face heat. "But…"

"What's the real problem?"

"I'm not in my twenties anymore, or even my thirties."

"Well, thank God for that. I don't want to be some old letch hitting on an infant."

"But…"

"Oh, I get it, you're worried about wrinkles and saggy skin and scars."

She nodded.

"We both have them honey, but that doesn't mean we can't enjoy each other." He leaned over the console and pulled her head toward him. His lips brushed the corner of her mouth in a soft kiss, and he continued the path, across her mouth to the other corner. It was a sweet, closed mouth kiss, but it still managed to send tingles of want through her.

She clutched at his shirt and pulled him back for another kiss. This one packed heat and desire. She opened her mouth and he swept inside, claiming her, dueling with her, ramping up the heat.

His hand moved and he cupped her breast, kneading it, the nipple beaded, and he ran his thumb over it. She gasped as fire shot through her.

He pulled back from the kiss. "Seems like everything is working just fine to me."

She opened her eyes, pulling slowly out of the drugged state she'd been in. It felt so damn good to have a man's hands on her curves. To hell with insecurities, she wasn't going to pass up this chance to have sex with a man who didn't see her as an authority figure. He saw her as a woman and that's all she wanted.

Carol glanced down at his crotch and saw his arousal pushing at his jeans, gratifying to her, it was clear he was on board. "I guess it is, let's go inside and explore a bit more. Leave the stuff, we'll get it later."

Max followed her in, and they went straight up to her room. She didn't pause to check on anything. It could all wait an hour. But mostly she didn't want the doubts creeping back in. When the door clicked shut and Max locked it, she gulped.

Before she could let nerves take over, Max pulled her into his arms and kissed her long and slow, his tongue exploring every inch of her mouth, creating little tornados of arousal that spun along nerve endings all throughout her body. Many of those tiny tornados went straight south congregating in her girl parts, reminding her just how much she had enjoyed sex.

When her husband had died unexpectedly, she'd been thrown into the mayor's office and had three young kids to raise, she'd been too busy to think of sex, too heartbroken to try again with another man. By the time she'd gotten into a routine and she'd come to terms with being alone, she'd become an authority figure in town and there weren't that many single men her age to begin with, so she just put her sexuality to the side, pleasuring herself if she had the urge.

Max, however, was reminding her of everything she'd missed. His hands slid down and cupped her butt, drawing her close where his arousal came into contact with her needy flesh. Less clothes would be good.

As if she'd spoken out loud, Max slid his hands under her shirt, hands moving over the skin of her back and sides as he pushed the shirt up her body and over her head. He dropped it on the back of a chair and looked down at her lace covered bra. She didn't wear scraps of lace like the younger generation could get away with, but even a good supportive bra could be pretty.

"Nice," he breathed out. He reached around to the back, his hands coming to a stop on the clasp. "Do you mind if I…"

"Not at all, please do." If he didn't free her heavy breasts and her hard nipples from the confines of her bra she might explode.

He unhooked the back and pulled the straps down her arms. He sucked in a breath as he pulled it away from her body. "Beautiful." He lifted both her breasts, one in each hand, testing the weight and squeezing gently. Then he ran his thumbs back and forth across her nipples and sensation shot straight through her.

He lowered his head and took one turgid peak into his mouth where he licked and sucked and bit down gently, while his hand mimicked his mouth on the other nipple. Her knees turned to water and she sagged.

He lifted his head and her nipple came free with a pop. He backed her over to the bed and gently pushed her down on it, joining her and immediately moving onto the other breast. He gave it the same attention and she was glad she wasn't trying to support herself, because she was rather certain all her bones were liquefying. And she still had her pants on, and he was fully dressed. She might not live through this encounter—but she was certain—it was going to be glorious.

Max was enjoying the hell out of Carol's tits, he'd always been a breast man, but he could admit hers were magnificent, full and round and perfect. They also seemed to be quite sensitive, which was sometimes unusual for well-endowed women. But he could feel her response to his ministrations, so he let himself enjoy.

Carol panted and said, "Max, stop. I can't take any more."

Max looked up letting the nipple he was suckling slide through his teeth and saw Carol's eyes nearly roll back in her head in ecstasy. "But you're enjoying it."

"It's… it's too much. You're still dressed, and I have my pants on. I want more. More skin. Your skin, next to mine."

He wanted to prolong this; he knew if he was naked it would be over too soon. So, he went to kiss her, to distract her a little longer.

She turned her face away and ground out. "Now Max! Naked. Both of us."

He sighed and stood to comply with her wishes. She started to take off her pants but then stopped to watch him disrobe. He was almost surprised by the look on her face as he removed his shirt and then unbuckled his pants. Max knew his body was in good shape for an old guy. He deliberately kept it that way so he could go hiking when he wanted to. Even ran in an occasional marathon. Not for speed or to win, but just to know he could accomplish it.

Carol apparently liked what she saw, her eyes had widened, and her pupils had dilated. She was fixated on his chest and abs. Pretty impressive feat, to have a woman ogling him at his age, made him feel like superman, and made his dick pulse to be out of his jeans.

Max pushed his pants down his legs taking the briefs with them and saw her lick her lips. His cock jumped and she gave him a sultry smile which caused his dick to jump again. She grinned at that and he growled stalking toward her.

"I'm naked now, let's finish getting you that way." He took hold of her waistband and she lifted her hips without being told, so he could whisk the jeans along with her panties, down her legs. When she was completely bare to him, he hummed in appreciation. She was amazing, so gorgeous. Her curves were perfect. He wanted to taste them, stroke them and enjoy every inch.

The shadow between her legs called to him, so he climbed back on the bed, pulled her knees apart, and made himself at home between her legs. He would taste the rest of her later, but right now he was going to taste her very center. He kissed that shadowy place and then pulled her folds open and licked.

Carol's hips raised off the bed and she nearly screamed at his first lick. If he thought her nipples were sensitive, they had nothing on her clit. He licked her again and she moaned, so he settled in—to feast—drinking in each sound that escaped her lips as he pleasured her.

She was thrashing and gripping the sheets in a death grip when she came with a scream that shook the rafters. He hoped all her guests were out of the building, rather than them calling the police about a murder being committed.

The woman lay panting, covered in a light sheen of sweat, not moving. Max sat back on his heels loving what he'd just done to her. His cock begged to continue, to slide into her hot, dripping channel, but he ignored it.

After long minutes, her blue eyes opened slowly, and a satisfied smile curved her lips. "That was amazing."

"You're welcome, and so far, no one has called the police from your screaming."

"I didn't scream."

He raised his eyebrows. "My ears are still ringing. I'm sure your throat is sore."

She swallowed then turned a bright scarlet, he watched in fascination as the color started in her cheeks and slowly spread down her neck and torso.

"My throat is a little scratchy," she admitted sheepishly.

"It was, by far, the best sound I've heard in years. It made me feel like a superhero."

She smiled and shook her head as the color receded from her body. "No, your mouth makes you a god, in my book."

He chuckled and preened, making her laugh.

She looked pointedly at his cock. "But we're not done yet.

The condoms are in the drawer, let's move on to the next event."

His cock leapt at her words, so he didn't hesitate to comply with her request. He rolled on a condom he found in the drawer, along with a dozen others, and wondered just what she'd been thinking, having so many on hand. He wasn't a kid anymore; it took him a while to recharge. Had she bought a giant economy sized box?

Not wanting to think about that, he climbed back on the bed and again fit himself between her legs. She didn't hesitate, but took him in hand and guided him into her hot wet body. She was tight, so he moved in slowly until he was fully seated.

While he waited for her body to stretch and get used to the feel of him inside, he kissed her with drugging kisses. When she put one leg around his waist and the other around his leg, he figured that was the signal to move, so he did.

Moving inside her slowly, making sure he was hitting her most sensitive areas, he slid in and out, over and over. She clutched at his arms and when he sensed she was getting close he moved faster, still careful to hit her pleasure points. Her body bowed up to his and she came, calling his name, her inner muscles squeezing him, dragging him along in her wake to completion. As his body emptied into hers, and pure pleasure shot through him, he groaned out her name.

He rolled them to their side, not wanting to squish her. He wasn't a little guy.

She opened her eyes, pushed his sweaty hair off his forehead, and looked deep into him. Then she smiled. "That was so much better than I remember. You might have made me an addict."

He thought of the drawer full of condoms and didn't like the idea of anyone else using them except him. But he wasn't going to be here long. He was, by golly, going to give using those up his best shot, however. He'd been just as amazed at their chemistry as she was.

"Well, I'll do my best to oblige you any time you want to indulge."

She smiled and let her eyes drift closed.

CHAPTER TWENTY-TWO

*C*arol was determined not to act weird with Max, after spending the night in his arms. She'd drifted off after their first sexual encounter. After a nap, they'd woken up and had called the Korean barbeque, to have them deliver food. Since it was summer and high season, they would deliver. Most of the year they did not.

They'd eaten in her room at her tiny table, she'd pulled on a dressing robe and he'd gone down to get the food in jeans and a t-shirt. Max had reported back that nothing had gone amiss with her not standing by, at least from what he could tell by the quietness of the house.

After they'd eaten, she had wondered if she should go down and man the fort, so to speak, but Max had distracted her with another round of love making. So, she'd decided if anyone needed her, they would find her. She'd left Max passed out in her bed this morning, to get downstairs in time to feed her guests.

She was so busy thinking about how she was not going to act weird around Max, that she startled when Judy came in to help her get the breakfast on.

Carol whirled around at the sound of someone coming in the kitchen. "Oh, Judy, you startled me."

"Sorry. You don't normally jump, when I come in, you must have been thinking hard. Anything I can help with?"

Carol waived her hand in what she hoped was a carefree manner, but probably looked like a marionette with tangled strings. She wasn't going to get into any personal disclosures with the high school girl who helped her in the mornings. Although people Judy's age probably didn't get all weirded out about sleeping with a man. "No nothing important. I think that pineapple is finally ripe enough to cut up for the morning fruit offerings."

Judy looked at her for one long moment and then turned to gather up the fruit.

Carol wondered if she had a big fat sign on her forehead announcing to the world, that she'd slept with Max last night. Now she was just being silly. She went back to concentrating on breakfast, the more she thought about not being weird, the weirder she got.

Max woke up alone—in Carol's room—that combination of facts was enough to make his head spin. She could have woken him when she needed to get up and get the breakfast on. He would have gone on to his own room, without batting an eye at the request. He'd figured when they drifted off, that she would do just that. But she hadn't, and he'd not woken when she got up, which also kind of surprised him. He wasn't a heavy sleeper. He chuckled at himself, she'd worn him out he supposed.

But now he had a dilemma, it was late enough in the day that if he walked out of her room and up the stairs he might run into guests and his disheveled appearance would tell its own story. He didn't really care what people thought of him, but he didn't want to bring any censure on Carol.

The alternative was to use her shower. He'd still be dressing in yesterday's clothes, but people probably wouldn't notice that. The problem with that idea was she always smelled pretty, and he assumed it was from her bath products. He didn't think he wanted to smell like a woman all day.

Quite the conundrum.

He finally decided the walk of shame was the better option, he didn't want to use her towels and bath products. He finger combed his hair with some water to get it to behave at least to some degree. He washed his face and hands. There was no remedy for his dirty clothes. He just needed to get to the stairs without anyone seeing him come out of Carol's room and he would be home free.

He opened the door and peered out. He didn't see anyone, and it seemed quiet to him. So maybe everyone on the floor had left already. He could hear the distant buzz of conversation and the tinkle of forks on plates.

Deciding it was now or never, he inched the door open and practically sprinted to the stairs, taking them two at a time until he reached his floor and charged down the hall to his room. He unlocked the door hastily and moved in quickly. Locking the door behind him, he breathed a sigh of relief. He'd made it and he didn't think anyone had seen him.

He vowed that the next time Carol and he spent the night together they would make better plans for the morning. Them spending the night in his room would be best, since it was her inn, and she could be on any floor at any time without arousing suspicion. But he didn't know if her hip could take it. She favored it a bit and it wasn't as flexible as it could be, but it had only been a year since her surgery and sometimes the stiffness took a while to go away.

Not wanting to miss breakfast, he hurried through

getting ready for the day. As he headed down the stairs—at a much leisurely pace than he'd come up—he thought about what they would need to get to the next clue. Gardening tools to clear away the heavy vine covering the cellar door. Possibly a small ladder to get down inside and the flashlights and lanterns, and the rest of their box of tricks, just in case.

Just before he entered the dining room, he wondered if he should greet Carol as a lover or the inn keeper. Probably the later, she might not want anyone to see a change in their relationship. Maybe he could give her fingers a quick squeeze, to show affection that she would notice, but no one else would.

With that plan in place he moved into the dining room and saw the lovely lady in question on the far side of the room talking to a family. She had an air about her that was welcoming and kind, regardless if she was talking to a family with rambunctious kids wanting to hurry through breakfast to get to the amusement park, or an older couple celebrating their fiftieth anniversary. It was a gift, that kind of connection to people and he loved to watch her stopping by each table making each and every guest feel special.

Max filled his plate and moved to his normal table; it was funny how people got into the habit of sitting in the same place day after day. Carol glanced at him and gave him a smile before turning back to the family with cheeks that had a bit more color in them. He didn't mind at all putting that pinkness in her cheeks.

She excused herself and came toward his table. Max noticed a bit of wariness in her gaze as she sat at his table like she'd done many mornings, so they could plan out their day.

Her coffee cup shook just a little as she placed it on the table, and he guessed she was feeling a little insecure about them this morning. He gave her his best smile and waved at his breakfast. "You've outdone yourself again."

Carol shook her head. "Not really, phyllo dough out of the freezer, some cream cheese, and fruit."

He'd broken off a bite and put it in his mouth and moaned in delight. "It's delicious."

Max reached across the table and squeezed her fingers for just a moment. "Relax. It's just you and me. Nothing needs to change between us. We still have a treasure to find."

Carol looked around and then whispered, "Well except for the sex. You don't feel odd about that, this morning?"

Max chuckled. "Odd? No not at all. Happy and relaxed. Other than trying to get to my room without anyone being the wiser, I found the last twenty-four hours to be excellent in every way. And I hope to repeat it again today. Other than the part where Nolan scowled at us for disturbing his evidence."

That got a small giggle out of her and she relaxed. "He was quite disgusted by us, wasn't he?"

"He was. I was thinking today we need to get down into the cellar, but there is a massive vine all over the top of the door. Do you have any hedge trimming shears?"

She relaxed completely as she thought it over. "I mostly hire out my yard work, but there might be some in the garage from back when my husband kept up the yard."

He raised his eyebrows. "From thirtyish years ago?"

"Well yes, but Terry kept up the yard while he was at home. So, they might not be in terrible shape."

"I'll investigate. A small ladder might be good to take, also."

"I think we had a five-foot ladder. I've not used it, but there might be one."

"If I need to, I'll go back to the hardware store and see what they have. Other than that, we'll just need what we've been taking all along."

CHAPTER TWENTY-THREE

$\mathcal{C}$arol finished packing them a lunch and some drinks, they were determined to find the last clue to the void and hopefully discover it. Max had stopped in to say he'd found hedge shears that were in sufficient shape for the job they were going to use them for. He'd said they'd only needed a squirt or two of the lubricant.

A ladder on the other hand was not available. "There *is* a ladder out there, but it's so decrepit I wouldn't even attempt to use it."

"Well I haven't used one in years, but I suppose it would be a good idea to have a ladder, just in case."

"There might be something already in the cellar, but if it was wood it will be in about the same shape as your ladder. We could go look and see if we need one before we buy something."

"But if we do that, we won't be able to go in, today. No go buy a ladder. If a person can walk around in there, we probably need a six foot one, don't you think?"

"Yeah, I doubt it's much deeper than that."

"Then go buy one. Do they have them at the little

outfitter place?" Carol asked, their little town didn't always have everything someone would want at any given moment. A ladder didn't seem like something they would necessarily have on hand. she could probably call around and find one to borrow, but she didn't really want to. It would bring what they were doing to light.

"Yeah, I saw a couple of ladders last time I was in there."

She relaxed then laughed at herself. Max buying a ladder and all the other things he'd purchased on her tab, probably had people talking anyway. But she hoped they thought he was helping around the house. If they could just get to the bottom of the mystery, then she would start on the house in earnest. Once she started hiring gardeners and cleaning people and the electrician and plumber, the word would be out, but she wasn't quite there, yet. "Good. I would rather not have to ask around to borrow one."

Carol had watched him leave, it was a fine sight to behold. She'd had to shake herself to get back to the task at hand, which was taking care of her other guests.

The rest of the morning had passed quickly, and all her guests were out enjoying the summer day. Karen had been there to help her clean up the rooms and common areas.

Carol had gotten a wild hair and had run upstairs and put two condoms in her jean pockets. It was silly to think of them making love anywhere except here at the inn, but if the opportunity arose, she didn't want to be without protection. She'd already gone through the change, but pregnancy was not the only reason to use something. Not that she had anything, and she doubted Max did either, but it didn't hurt to be cautious.

She was as prepared as she could be, when Max came back into the house. "You ready?"

"Yes, do you think we'll find it today?"

"We've got a good shot at it. It's early and we already have the first two items. But we'll have to see what we discover underground. There could be a lot more problems outside, that we haven't encountered indoors."

Carol nodded. "I can see that. But I just have a feeling we'll get there today."

"I have to admit to an air of expectancy myself. Shall we?" He waived his hand toward the door, she grabbed the lunch, he took hold of the cooler and they hurried out to the car.

Max said, "Let's store the food in the library, since that's our ultimate destination."

"Good idea. I'll do that while you take the shears and the ladder to the back and start chopping away at the vine."

Carol stored everything in the library and hurried out to find Max hacking away at the vine. The vine was, in fact, several different types that had coiled themselves together. Some particularly hardy weeds looked to be coiled around a pumpkin or cucumber vine. The weeds were entangled around everything and were the primary difficulty.

Max had to chop through the pumpkin vine also, due to the mess the vines had become. The poor guy was working hard to try to free the entrance. He was making some headway, but it was slow going.

Carol waited in breathless anticipation to discover what was being kept below ground. When Max finally crowed in triumph, she was on her feet in a second to see if he'd managed to get the door clear.

Max opened the cellar door and looked inside, surprised to find it cement, with actual steps leading down inside. "I guess we didn't need the ladder after all." He said sheepishly.

Carol nudged him to the side and laughed. "Wow, I never would have guessed."

Max propped the heavy door up, and proceeded her down the steps, calling out in joy when he reached the bottom. "Come on down, it's perfectly safe, and even dry. Not at all what I was expecting."

Carol took hold of her flashlight in a death grip and went down the surprisingly clean stone steps and into the main room. She looked around and was surprised to see bottles of wine and all kinds of canned produce. "This is amazing. I'll bet that wine is delicious. Not so sure I would want to eat what's in the cans and jars however."

Max grinned at her expression. "Glad to see I wasn't the only one surprised, let's go down one more level."

There were stone stairs to the next level also and down there they found bins for produce and what had formerly been a meat locker of sorts. But there were also furnishings in one corner. That's what pulled at them.

Max felt a surge of excitement when he saw the draped and wrapped items in the corner. It looked like some chairs and a table were stored, but he also saw several things that looked like paintings wrapped securely in protective wrap.

"Rather than open these paintings down here, I think we should take them upstairs to unwrap."

Carol nodded, it looked like about a half dozen paintings were standing on one side of a chair. "I agree. I'm going to make sure there isn't another level down."

While Carol checked for more secrets, Max hauled out the first load of paintings and took them into the house. Placing them in the library, he went out to get the second load.

"Find anything?" he called out when he got back.

Carol was peering into one of the barrels. "No, just some very old potatoes."

Max grinned at her. "I don't think we'll need those. I can

carry the rest of the paintings if you can grab our supplies. I already put the ladder back in your car."

They pulled the house painting off the wall, finding another little door behind it with another piece of metal. Max put that into his pocket along with the other one and they took the house painting into the library and set it next to Little Boy Blue.

Turning on the last group of paintings, Carol said, "Let's get started."

There were six paintings all carefully wrapped, the outer layer was plastic and then inside was heavy duty oil cloth.

Max muttered, "Why did they go to so much trouble to preserve them and then put them in the cellar? Of course, it was the nicest cellar I've ever seen, but why not just keep them in the house?"

Carol said, "Maybe just to keep all the clues separated. Let's open all of them first and then look to see which one is for the last clue."

Max was glad she had suggested that, once they got all six of them unwrapped, because every single picture had a dragon in it. Some were famous paintings like Saint George and the Dragon, a William Blake Red Dragon with the Woman Clothed with the Sun, and a Japanese dragon. He was surprised to see a picture of Puff the Magic Dragon, of all things. The last two he didn't recognize, which didn't mean much, as he wasn't a dragon enthusiast.

Carol shook her head. "How are we supposed to know which is the right one? Their frames are all very similar, they are all about the same size."

"I have no idea." He looked at each of the paintings in puzzlement. At first, he was tempted to cross off Puff the Magic Dragon, but he didn't actually have a good reason to do that. "Guess this is the last piece of the challenge. Did you bring the letter and the poem?"

"Yes." She pulled it out of a pocket in the lunch container. "Do you want to eat while we examine them for more clues?"

"Not yet, maybe a granola bar. I was thinking we could eat once we got inside the room. Kind of like a reward for winning. Of course, if we don't figure it out and we get too hungry, I won't protest."

Carol laughed. "I was kind of holding out for that idea, too." She shrugged. "I went a little overboard on the food, probably brought more than we can eat. But I wanted to celebrate finding the void."

"Then let's get to figuring this out."

Carol handed him the two letters, the regular one and the hidden message one he'd transcribed. Carol kept the poem, reading it over again.

Max didn't see anything special in the letter regarding the dragon other than they were in the bottom level of the cellar, which is where they had found them.

He glanced up and saw Carol look at the poem and then each of the paintings. "What did you find?"

"It says, *Where is the dragon that's guarding the keep?* I took that to mean the void, but now I'm wondering about that. In the St George picture, the dragon is dead, so he's not guarding anything."

Max saw where she was going with this and figured it was as good a trail to go down as any other. "Blake's dragon is referring to scripture and is a bad dragon, so he's after the woman and also not guarding anything."

"Exactly. The Japanese dragon is just chilling above the ocean. Now Puff, he in a sense guarded Jackie Paper's youth and all his childish treasures, so I think he's a possibility."

"I agree, at first I thought to cross him off since most of the depictions of Puff is a cartoon. This one isn't a cartoon and is more realistic, but everything around him clearly shows it's Puff."

Carol looked at the last two. "That Chinese dragon is in front of some temple, so he could be guarding it. Or he could be going to destroy it. Hard to say from the picture. But I say we keep it."

"Okay and the last one? It's clearly a home-painted dragon, maybe by someone in the family. But I can't see that it's guarding anything."

"Yeah, but since it might be a family thing let's keep it in the back of our mind. Now what are we supposed to do with them?"

Max nodded toward an empty wall at the far end of the room. "My guess is we hang them down there. Let's see if there are hooks."

"It's kind of a funny alcove to hang them in, but let's do it and see. I'll get the first one, you get the second and then we'll bring the three choices down for the third."

Max nodded but brought two paintings in two trips, while Carol looked at the wall.

Carol whirled on him when he brought the last two paintings. "There *are* hooks. The middle one is higher than the other two. But I think you can reach it."

Max hung the first two paintings and they debated the third.

Carol tapped a finger to her lips. "Let's start with the home-painted one."

Max nodded; he honestly didn't have a preference. He hung the last one and they stepped back. He didn't see a damn thing to give them a clue. Apparently, Carol did, because she gasped.

"There is a gold thread running through the first two, but not the third. Try the Chinese dragon."

He still didn't see it but switched out the painting as directed.

"Come back here, you seem to be blocking the light source that shows the gold."

He walked back to her and looked carefully. He bent down to her level and did see a faint glimmer in the first two, but not the third. "Let's try Puff."

He hurried back and switched the painting to Puff. As he did so there was a faint click. He looked toward the wall that the sound had come from, it was a bookshelf, he didn't see anything else, so he hurried back to Carol.

This time when he bent down, he saw the glow on all three paintings. He followed the line to the wall where the click had come from and saw a tiny golden glow the size of a pin hole. On one particular book in the shelf.

Carol whispered, "Do you see the dot on that book?"

"I do. Keep your eyes on it, so we don't lose which book it is."

They both walked slowly to the bookshelf. The dot disappeared from sight, but they both pointed to the same book. It was a book about libraries, of all things. "I hope it's more than just an instruction manual on how to run a library."

Carol sighed but didn't take her eyes from the book. "I am going to be sorely disappointed if it is just that."

"Let me get some flashlights."

"Bring the rest of our stuff nearer, while you're at it."

Max held the flashlights and had put his backpack of emergency tools back on. While Carol carefully pulled the book off the shelf. He was disappointed that it was just a book on running libraries. Carol laid it on a nearby table and they peered into the vacant spot with a flashlight.

"There might be something back there, pull out a couple more books."

Carol pulled out one of nursery rhymes, and another about dragons, and a third about Queen Anne architecture. With those four significant books pulled out, they could see a handle. Carol tried to turn it, but it didn't budge. "Nothing, you try."

Max handed her his flashlight and he tried. It didn't turn for him either, but he felt movement. "I'm not sure it turns at all, but I felt something give." Rather than trying to turn it he attempted pulling on it, but nothing happened. Then he tried pushing and that's when it moved.

Carol squealed. "An accordion book shelf. How cool is that!"

Max was surprised at how the bookshelves had moved. The middle, between two, came out in the room and the edge of the one they were fiddling with slid along a track. Whoever had designed this building was very clever.

Carol sighed, when there was another door behind that one. "It needs a key."

Max pulled the keyring out of its spot in his backpack and handed it to her. "Isn't there one we haven't found a use for? Try it."

She did and the key slid in easily, but wouldn't turn. "It won't turn."

"Let me look." Max looked closely at the mechanism and grinned. "I think I know."

He pulled the two pieces of metal, that had been behind the first two paintings, out of his pocket and fit them into the plate like puzzle pieces, slight clicks accompanied each fitting. The key turned easily after that and they pushed the door open.

They shone their flashlights into the room. It was not at all what they were expecting. Max gathered up their lunch and supplies and they went into the room. The void had been found!

CHAPTER TWENTY-FOUR

arol walked into the enormous room, that seemed to have its own light source. It was not pitch black like she had been expecting. She looked up and up and up, shocked to see the center of the room extended all four stories, which is where the light was coming from. It was coming through what they had thought might be a bell tower, or clock tower. The light was then reflected downward by strategically placed mirrors.

That was a marvel in itself, but it was not the only one. The walls were filled with books and it looked like each floor had rows of shelves that were also filled. There had to be thousands of books in this one room, just on this one level, not to mention the other three.

The Zimmermans had not just left a building, they'd left a library. Granted, newer books would need to be purchased. But this was one heck of a start.

Max came up behind her and whistled. "Well I'll be damned, look at all those books. And the light in this room is incredible."

He walked past her and set the lunch and their supplies

on a little table, next to a stack of thick books. On top of the books was an envelope addressed to Carol. Max handed her the envelope and set the keys on the table by the books.

She read the letter out loud, "Dear Carol, We are so happy you persevered to solve our little puzzles. You are standing amongst our most treasured possessions. When we had to move from our home, we knew there was no way we could take all this with us, and we wanted the town to reap the benefit of our love for books. Words are important, they can mean so much. You will find books for all ages and types of readers, over half the books are non-fiction on every subject we could imagine. The fiction books range from children's story books to thriller to romance. We've left you money for both renovating the house as needed, to make it a library and community center, and to purchase new books. The lawyers knew about part of it, but there is another account at the bank in Chelan in your name, the safe deposit box that this key fits will give you the passbook. We plan to keep purchasing books, so you'll probably have more books arriving after we die. We'll make sure they are carefully protected and put into those pod things. So, it won't hurt them to stay in the pods until the renovation is complete. The books under the letter have a history of Chelan and Chedwick. You will be able to read about how our families are connected in the top one. Thank you so much for carrying out our dream and legacy. If you wouldn't mind, we would like the library to be named The Zimmerman Library. Sincerely, Sam and Matilda Zimmerman."

Her throat tightened and she couldn't speak anymore. Max handed her a bottle of water and she smiled her thanks through a haze of tears.

She put the letter back into the envelope and Max put it in his backpack for safekeeping. Then they looked at the stack of books on the table. She would take those home and start on the top one.

There was a sound at the door, and they turned to see a man standing there with a gun drawn. He looked familiar to Carol, it took her a minute to realize it was the legal courier, Joseph somebody, looking much more disheveled than he had standing on her front porch.

The man sneered. "I see you finally found the treasure room. It took you long enough."

Max frowned. "How did you get in here? We locked the doors."

He waved the gun at them. "Do you think I didn't copy all the keys and documents before I delivered them. I, Joseph James Jenkinson, am not a fool. I just didn't have all the clues you did."

"So, you were the one in here before?" Carol asked.

"Yes, of course. My grandfather designed this building, and he used to go on and on about all the clever things he had designed. Hidden doors, secret passageways, and an enormous treasure room. I've been waiting for years for those old farts to die, so I could be the courier to bring you the packet. I'm an excellent courier but it's a boring job and I planned to retire on the treasure in this room. Now put your hands up and back up."

Carol looked at Max who nodded slightly. She hoped he had some idea of how to get them out of this mess. They put their hands up and backed further into the room.

Triple J, as she was starting to call him in her mind, came into the room. With quick glances around, not taking his eyes off of them for more than a second or two, he took in the room. Then he walked in further and glanced up. "Books? The whole damn place is filled with books?"

He looked back at them in fury, his hands shaking so much she thought the gun might go off. He gestured around wildly with it. "I waited my whole life to get inside this trea-sure room and all it contains is musty fucking books?"

Carol nodded when his glare landed on her.

"God dammit. My whole life. That stupid job. Removing the first courier, so I could take his place, and the wonderful treasure is fucking books. Well hell, I would go shoot my grandfather right between the eyes if he wasn't already dead."

Max casually asked, "What do you mean by 'removed' the first courier?"

Joseph sneered. "Let's just say he's gone missing. Not to be found. I waited my whole adult life for this one job, and they were going to let some other guy do it. No way was I going to let that happen."

Carol felt ice flow through her veins. This man was a murderer and would shoot his own grandfather. *Dear God, how were they going to get out of this?*

Max gave her a warning *don't rile the man* look and she nodded her agreement. She was so glad he was with her, she didn't panic easily but this might be the perfect scenario to do so. She hoped and prayed they didn't die today.

That man is a moron, a dangerous moron, but a moron just the same. Max couldn't believe what was coming out of Joseph James Jenkinson's mouth. Didn't he have any clue he was giving them evidence of crimes he had committed? Or was he planning to kill them too, so they couldn't tell anyone? Well Max didn't intend to go down without a fight.

The temper tantrum finally started to wane, and Max wondered if that was a good thing or a bad thing.

"Fuck, now what am I going to do? I can't go back to that stupid job, since I sent them a resignation letter once I got here. Besides that, I hate it. I don't have any money and I just told these two idiots everything. I could shoot them I suppose, lock the houseback up, and go my merry way. I could even burn the damn thing down," Joseph muttered to himself.

Max and Carol shared a glance and Max tried to exude a calm he wasn't really feeling.

"No, maybe killing them isn't a good idea, that would just put two more people on my head, and she is the Mayor so someone might miss her and come after me. Maybe just lock them in this room. It would take time for them to be found. Yeah, that's better, but I still need money." He stopped muttering and looked up. "Give me all your money."

Max didn't want to comply, but if they cooperated, they might live through this. He had a couple hundred dollars for travelling money. "My wallet is in the front pocket of the backpack on the floor right there."

Joseph used one hand to dig it out, the other hand still holding the gun on them. He flipped it open. "Sweet, that will get me out of town on the damn ferry. How about you Miz Mayor?"

Carol squeaked, "I only have a couple of twenties in my pocket. I don't carry a lot of cash."

"Every little bit helps, hand it over, sister. And both of you give me your cell phones. I'll just leave them on the table in the foyer, while I vacate this crappy little town."

Damn, he'd been hoping the moron would forget about the phones. They handed them over and Max prayed he would just leave them and the keys.

Joseph looked at his watch. "And I have just enough time to get to the ferry, if I take your car, and don't have to walk the whole damn way. Keys." He held out his hand.

Carol handed him her car keys, and Max breathed a sigh of relief when he didn't ask for the others.

"Now you two, just have yourselves some fun reading all

these fucking books, while I remove myself from your idiotic presence."

He backed out the door, which swung shut, and Max heard the key turn in the lock. He glanced at the table and motioned to the keys, but put a finger to his lips so Carol stayed quiet. He heard the outer bookshelves move back into place and then heard a dragging sound that chilled his blood. If Joseph blocked the bookcase from folding outward, they might be truly trapped.

CHAPTER TWENTY-FIVE

*C*arol was determined not to panic. She'd never faced a gun-toting maniac, however, so she could admit to adrenaline pumping through her body. Anyone that didn't have that kind of reaction in the situation they'd just been in was either crazy or dead. Since she was neither she didn't see anything wrong.

The panic, however, had to do with the dragging sound they'd heard. When Max had directed her attention to the fact that Triple-J had left the keys she'd felt certain it would only take them a few minutes to get out of the room. But then she'd watched the tension ratchet up in Max's face at the sound of the dragging, and had drawn the same conclusion he had probably drawn.

Triple-J had moved something in front of the bookcase to keep it from opening. Once they knew it was safe, they would check that out. Max moved over near the door to listen at it, and she prayed Triple-J had truly decided not to burn the place down, and was indeed speeding down the road in her car to the ferry.

She didn't know what time it was, she didn't wear a watch

anymore, relying on her phone for that function. Even without her phone she didn't think there was a really long time until the ferry came, so she couldn't see the jerk waiting around. Asshole, taking her phone and her car, although once they got out of here, both of those items would be waiting for her, she hoped.

Carol had no intention of thinking that they might not get out. It was not a matter of *if* they got out, but when. In the morning when she didn't show up for breakfast, Judy would sound the alarm. Nolan and her kids knew she was coming out here, so they would come to look.

Thank goodness, Nolan had been out here, and would know to search on a deeper level, knowing about the secrets. She was fairly certain she'd mentioned they were searching for the void to her kids, and Nolan, for that matter.

Finally, it looked like Max was certain Triple-J was gone, he walked back and took her hand. "Are you all right?"

"I'm fine, do you think it's safe?"

"Yes. It's been quiet long enough that I think he's gone."

"Then let's try the door and see if he put something in front of the bookcase."

Max frowned. "That's what I'm afraid of, too."

"Only one way to find out."

A few minutes later, their fears were verified. The bookcase wouldn't budge.

Max swore under his breath and Carol felt like kicking something. The adrenaline was starting to dissipate, and she felt cold and shaky. "I think I need to eat; my body is crashing."

"Yeah, mine too. Good thing we brought the food in here with us."

She opened the container, while Max got them out some drinks. "I'm glad I brought so much, now, in case we're here for a while."

"We should probably ration it, especially the water."

"I used bags of ice instead of the blue ice things. I forgot to freeze them last night. That will give us a bit more water as they melt."

"That's handy. After we eat, we need to explore this whole place. There might be an exit on one of the other floors."

Carol hoped that was true but didn't put a lot of faith in it. If there were multiple doors, she didn't think gaining entrance, in the first place, would have been such a challenge, but she wasn't going to mention that. "Wouldn't that be wonderful?"

Max looked at her for a long time—a far away look to his eyes—as she munched on the half of a ham sandwich she'd taken. She would save the other half for later. A few grapes would help with some quick sugar.

Max ate a few more bites. "I think him taking your car, might be a good thing."

"How so?"

"Well, if it's sitting at the ferry landing for hours, won't someone take notice and mention it to someone else, and the whole town will be wondering why, about fifteen minutes later?"

She laughed. "Well you might be right about that. I'm certain there will be a hue and cry when I don't show up for breakfast in the morning, Judy is certain to sound the alarm. All the kids know we've been coming out here, and Nolan of course. I think I've even mentioned us searching for this room. Although how they will find it…" She trailed off not wanting to continue the thought.

"I don't think it will be that hard. We left a pile of wrappings and all those extra paintings just hanging around in the library. It's the only room in the whole house that has anything weird or out of place in it."

She brightened. "Oh, I hadn't thought of that. And if they

find our cell phones in the foyer, they will know we are here. If they get in the door in the first place or even the gate, what if Triple-J locked them?"

Max huffed out a chortle. "Triple-J?"

Carol shrugged. "It seemed to fit. What an odd little man he was. Quite crazy, too."

"I don't think he'll get far, once we get out and tell Nolan everything. Couriers, like he is, probably have some kind of registration in case they take off with the loot. Plus, he's very proud of his name Joseph John Jenkinson."

"James, Joseph James Jenkinson. And you're right, he did bandy his name around quite often." She stood and went to put the rest of her sandwich back with the others.

"You didn't eat much."

"I ate enough for now. I would rather have several mini meals, than eat it all now and go hungry later. We don't know how long it will take them to find us."

"Good idea." Max put the rest of his sandwich back in the plastic bag and his half full water bottle back in the cooler. He hefted his backpack, placing the keys inside it, grabbed the flashlights, and her hand. "Let's explore."

Max didn't expect to find much, but looking around would give them something to do, rather than worry. So, he held Carol's hand as they started poking around on the first floor. They went around the walls and noticed some of the books as they went. It was an eclectic collection, and nothing was filed in any sort of order.

They looked all around the main floor and were surprised to find a tiny door in one corner.

Carol squeaked. "Look a door.".

Max pulled it open to find a tiny bathroom with only a toilet and a sink.

He felt Carol sag. "Not what I was hoping for."

"No, but if it works, it will make our imprisonment more comfortable."

"Oh. I didn't think of that aspect of being trapped."

Max turned on the sink and brown rusty water came out. "It might run clean after a while, but since we don't know the water source, or if the pipes are bad, let's save that for later."

The toilet also flushed although it acted a little sluggish. They both said in unison, "Emergency only."

They finished the circuit of the room without finding anything else interesting, and took the stairs to the second floor, which yielded nothing but more bookshelves, stuffed with books. The third floor was the same. The fourth floor which they had jokingly called the bell tower was a totally different story.

Carol gasped as Max stood frozen at the top of the stairs.

On the right side of the room were bookshelves, not ones that went all the way to the ceiling, but short ones, above those were windows that looked out over the lake and town. They could practically see all the way to Chelan.

But the surprising part of the room was on the left. It was a combination of reading room and he didn't know, a boudoir maybe. There were big, overstuffed chairs with footstools, a daybed, and a double wide chaise lounge. Tables were scattered around the chairs, some still had books piled on them, like their reader had just stepped away for a moment. Except that the furniture was covered with dust covers.

A refrigerator, coffee pot, and microwave sat in one corner next to a sink. On the other side of the sink was a bar with all kinds of liquor bottles, many of them half full, others were unopened. Next to that was a set of cupboards and he spied another small door that probably led to another bathroom.

Carol walked over to the cupboards and pulled them open to find them filled with food. Jars of pickles and jams. Cans of all kinds. And boxes of what was sure to be petrified crackers and other snacks.

Carol shut the doors and shuddered. "I'm not betting any of that is safe to eat."

Max laughed. "Probably not, but interesting to find."

Carol went over to the little door he assumed was another tiny bathroom and pulled open the door. She just stood there for a long time not moving and then called out to him. "Max? You are not going to believe this."

He stopped looking out the windows on this side of the building, that looked out over the mountains, and walked over to her.

He looked over her shoulder and whistled. "A person could live up here."

"It's huge. I was expecting a tiny one like below. Not a giant room with a huge two-person tub. There's even a small shower tucked in a corner, like an afterthought."

"It probably was a late addition. Most people in the US bathed until the fifties and sixties, when showers became more popular. New houses came with them before that, but this older house would have been retrofitted with one."

Max stepped out of the room and looked around again. "You know what? I think we should spend the night up here, if we end up waiting until morning. We can see the gate from here. It's not closed, so that's a plus."

Carol crossed over to the window he was looking out of. "Well that's a relief. Not that Terry wouldn't just get the fire department bolt cutter and chop right through the chain or lock, but it makes it more obvious we might be in here."

Max continued his thought. "This room will also give us

moon and starlight rather than being down there in the pitch dark. And the furniture is more comfortable. We've not yet found any rat or mice infestation, so I'm hoping that includes this floor. When you opened the cupboards, I didn't see any gnawed-on packages, did you?"

"No as a matter of fact I didn't. When we see the cavalry arriving, we can go back down. Do any of the windows open, so we can yell out of them?"

Max went all around the room checking, and found no windows that opened. That was disappointing, but probably also the reason the place was in such good condition. "Nope. So, do you want to stay up here tonight? I could go bring our stuff up and we can keep watch from here, rather than being clueless down below."

She nodded. "Yes, let's do that."

Max wondered how long it would be before someone found them. He was happy to be spending time with Carol, but the unknown future put a damper on everything. Including their success in finding the gigantic library.

CHAPTER TWENTY-SIX

*C*arol stood by the windows facing the gate, while Max brought up their food and supplies. She hoped that someone would notice that she and Max were missing tonight, but that seemed highly unlikely. If someone spotted her car at the landing it might raise some questions, but she doubted it would be enough to sound an alarm.

If Triple-J was smart, he wouldn't have driven up in it in the first place. Had she been the one trying to make a getaway, she would leave it a block or two away, so no one noticed her driving someone else's car. She hoped he hadn't been smart, and somebody had seen him leaving her car.

She sighed when her practical nature took over. No one would miss her until morning, when Judy came and found the kitchen empty and no preparation of breakfast for the guests. By the time Judy got there, looked around for her and called Sandy, who would come straight over to search the house, and finally call Nolan, Terry, and Janet to make sure they didn't know where she was, it would probably be at least nine before they made it out here. That was being optimistic.

Try as she might, she couldn't imagine a scenario where they might look for her today. She and Max would be spending the night in the house, that was almost certain. Maybe she and Max could make good use of the double lounger, if it didn't have any critters. The day bed could work too, but it was very narrow. Her face heated as she pictured it.

"Okay, I got everything up here."

She turned to look, and he held up the thick book that had been on the top of the pile downstairs. The history of Chedwick.

"I thought you might want to read this while we wait for rescue."

All right, he was clearly not on the same wavelength about how to spend their waiting time. Darn it.

"Great thanks. I kind of think we'll be here until mid-morning; it will take that long for Judy to sound the alarm and gather the troops."

Max nodded. "Those were my thoughts also. Hopefully, someone will feed your guests."

"Sandy knows I keep emergency coupons for Amber's restaurant or Samantha's bakery. Judy can hand them out. Not the best scenario, but no one will go hungry." She turned back to the windows. "Do you think we should stand guard and watch?"

"Maybe for a while, not all night."

"Yeah, that's what I was thinking too. Can you check the furniture, make sure they don't have critters?"

"Sure."

She noticed he thoroughly checked the double chaise lounge first. A small smile flitted across her lips. Maybe his thoughts weren't as far from hers as she had imagined.

"Lounger is good."

He moved to the day bed next, pulling it all apart to check

the mattresses, sheets, blankets, bedspread, and pillows. Then he carefully put everything back the way he had found it. It wasn't quite as neat, but passable. The dust covers he was putting in a pile out of the way of where they might need to walk.

"Daybed is good too. A little musty but the blankets will keep us warm if the temperature drops."

Carol said, "It shouldn't. I don't think they were predicting any storms."

"Good to know."

He checked the chairs and declared them fine also. Carol was beginning to wonder how this house had been abandoned for so many years, yet had no animal infestation other than a few spiders. She caught a flicker of something near the gate and she gasped.

Max hurried over, standing behind her and looking over the top of her head. "What did you see?"

She was staring intently and then it moved again. Her shoulders slumped. "Just a bird."

Max put his arms around her and drew her close. "It will be all right. They will find us tomorrow. We've just got a few hours. Let's pretend it's a secret rendezvous."

Carol laughed, but it sounded weak and insincere. She put her head back on his shoulder as he held her from behind and tried to relax.

Max was finding it hard to keep up a good front for Carol. It wasn't that he didn't believe they would be found. He had confidence in Nolan and his ability to make correct assumptions. They had enough food and water to last them until tomorrow, so he wasn't concerned about that.

What made him boiling mad was letting that little twerp

get the drop on them. Yes, he had a gun and was clearly unstable, but it still pissed him off that he had just stood there and let the guy take their phone, their money, Carol's car, and then lock them in the damn hidden room.

He should have done *something* to protect Carol. But no, he'd been a chickenshit and now it ate at him, especially since she was upset.

"Max, what's wrong?"

"Nothing," he growled out. Dammit he'd gone stiff with anger. He relaxed his body and the arms he had around her.

"I call bullshit on that one. You were stiff as a board and practically vibrating." She turned in his arms and looked in his eyes. "Tell me."

"Nothing,"

"Tell me."

He sighed, she was not going to let this go. "Fine, I'm pissed off that I let that pitiful excuse for a man lock us in here and walk away."

"He had a gun and was waiving it around. It was safer to let him walk away. You heard him, he'd already killed people. He would have thought nothing about shooting us, if we'd tried anything,"

"Yeah, but—"

"Yeah, but nothing. The man was crazy. It would have been a hell of a lot worse to be locked in here with one of us bleeding."

"I know. I do. But I still feel like I failed you. You're worried and I don't like it."

She put her hands on his face, forcing him to look her in the eye. "I'm not that worried. In fact, I was thinking about the two of us enjoying the lounger."

"You were?"

"Yes, but you brought up that huge book to read."

Max chuckled. He was totally on board with christening

the lounger. "We can carry the book back downstairs unread."

"Then kiss me, Max."

"You don't think we should watch the gates?"

"No, we can check once in a while, we can see the parking area in front of the house. Besides I really don't think anyone will be looking for me until morning. We've been keeping ourselves occupied in the evenings." She waggled her eyebrows at him, like he did to her sometimes.

It was adorable. He laughed and pulled her close. Her body melted against his and he decided maybe it wasn't such a bad thing to have the rest of the day and all night to themselves.

CHAPTER TWENTY-SEVEN

*C*arol woke with a warm man wrapped around her. It was early morning, still dark, but with just a hint of daylight on the eastern edge of the horizon. He was spooning her, keeping her back toasty warm. She would normally be in her kitchen by now, bustling around getting the baked goods and the coffee started. She laid there and thought about all that had happened to lead up to this morning, where she would watch the world wake up slowly.

They were on the chaise lounge, they'd found more sheets stored in plastic bags in a closet, so they'd used those rather than the ones from the day bed. She had condoms in her pocket, so they were able to put them to use. They'd drawn out the lovemaking, since they were in no rush.

They'd touched and kissed and tasted until both of them were ready to explode, ramped higher than they'd ever gone before, which made the final destination so much stronger. For a couple of old farts, they'd done a damn fine job of making the earth shake. Those young kids had nothing on them, her generation knew how to build toward satisfaction. Delayed gratification was earth shattering.

After the first round, they'd had more of the food and drinks, both of them wrapped in sheets, rather than getting fully dressed. They'd read for a while until there was no more sunlight, even from the long summer days.

The history of Chedwick was fascinating, she'd heard a lot of passed down stories, but this was a much more detailed accounting. She hadn't gotten to the connection between the Zimmermans and Andersons yet, but both families had been mentioned in the earliest pages of the book, so it was only a matter of time.

Max had found a book on Victorian Architecture he'd never seen before. He'd poured over it to see if his assumptions about load-bearing walls matched the books descriptions. Only one area differed from what he'd thought, but it would be easy to make those changes in his designs.

When it got too dark to read, they had lit one of the lanterns, but hadn't wanted to light more in case they needed it later. She'd shivered at that thought because it would mean they'd not been found. They were being careful with their food and water, but it wouldn't last forever.

After talking over what they'd read they eventually decided to climb back in their bed for the night, which had resulted in another long slow sexual journey. Possibly more powerful than the last, and then they'd dropped into sleep.

Now she lay in the early morning, hoping to be found. As comfortable as the night had been, she wanted to go home. She wanted to get up in the early morning and bake. She wanted her freedom. She did not enjoy the feeling of being trapped.

"What are you thinking about?" said a deep growling voice in her ear. "You've gotten all tense."

"It's nothing. I just... I just hope they find us this morning. I've discovered I'm not comfortable with confinement."

"I have every confidence in your kids and Nolan. He

seemed like an intelligent man and he knew we were still trying to find the hidden room."

She sighed. "I know… it's just… it took us almost a week."

Max nuzzled her neck, sending waves of pleasure dancing along her skin.

"True, but we did all the hard part. All they have to do is find the library and move whatever that twit put in front of the bookcase. If we see them drive in, maybe we can yell through the wall and give them instructions. It isn't completely sound-proofed."

Max went back to nuzzling her neck which made it hard for her to think through his words. But he was right, they had found all the clues and lined them up. It wasn't quite as simple as he was trying to make it sound, but it wouldn't take a week either, especially if there were a few of them. They could split up and search faster.

She put her worries away and turned to enjoy the man in her temporary bed.

Max was going to do his very best to take the fear from Carol. He could admit to being concerned himself, but at the same time he was ninety nine percent certain they would be out of the library by noon. That was still several hours from now. They wouldn't even know she was missing for a couple more.

So, he could distract her for a while and then they would get up. Clean up their mess and start standing watch at the window. He didn't think she had any more condoms with her, but he could still find plenty of ways to take her mind off her doubts.

Starting with her delectable neck, that was right there in front of him. He gave it little kisses and nibbles, starting just below her ear and continuing down to where her neck met her shoulder. He enjoyed that soft spot, until he felt tremors. Good, he was getting through to her.

He had just started moving his hand toward her breast when she flipped in his arms, so she was facing him, that hand could now cup her ass. Not at all a bad alternative. He loved her perfectly round butt.

Her mouth reached up to his, and he was more than happy to let her kiss him. In fact, she didn't get very far into it before he hauled her close, and took the kiss from warm to steamy in seconds. She moaned low in her throat as he pulled her up against his body and deepened the kiss at the same time. The kiss went on and on, until they ran out of air, and had to break apart. He kissed her cheeks and nose and eyelids, then went back to her mouth for another long, wet kiss.

He started kissing down her body, spending a long time on her breasts, kissing, suckling, squeezing. She squirmed as he kept up the torture for long minutes.

"Max."

Her nipple popped out of his mouth when he looked up. "What, sweetheart?"

"Stop the torment."

"But I'm having fun."

"Max."

"All right, if you insist." He moved lower on her body kissing his way down her stomach.

"Max."

He looked up and raised an eyebrow in question.

"I was wanting you inside me."

"You don't have any more condoms, love."

She squirmed again as he kissed her belly heading lower toward the damp curls. She grabbed his hair and clutched, holding him still for a moment. "I don't care. We're both clean. I've gone through the change. There is nothing to worry about."

"Well, if you insist."

She relaxed at his words, letting go of his hair, but he was determined, so he swooped in to taste her. And then she didn't have the strength or willpower to stop him from enjoying her fully.

After she'd screamed his name in climax, he gladly joined with her, to continue to pleasure her with his extremely hard dick. Her hot, wet core caressed him until they were both on the verge of ecstasy. She grabbed his ass and held on, as they went soaring.

As their bodies cooled, he pulled the sheets back up over them and she drifted into sleep again. He felt her body soften, and before he joined her in slumber, he congratulated himself on distracting her from worrying.

CHAPTER TWENTY-EIGHT

*C*arol woke again cuddled up with a warm man, this time she was slung across his chest, their legs tangled together, her head on his shoulder. It was later, but still early, the light had that pink hue of dawn. Judy would be arriving at the inn at any time.

They should probably get up and get ready to face the day. She had the confidence that her family and friends would find them. Moving off of Max was not an enticing idea, she was quite comfortable. She could stay like that for hours, but she didn't want her kids, or Nolan for that matter, to find them in this particular state.

She started to untangle herself and Max opened one eye. "What's up? I like you being my blanket."

"I like it too, but Judy will be waking everyone up any minute and we should probably be dressed when they come to save us."

Max growled, "I suppose, but they might not get here for hours."

"True, but I want to straighten up the place, too. I'll take the sheets we used home to wash them." Her stomach growled. "And maybe we should eat something."

Max chuckled. "Yeah I'm kind of starving from all your amorous activity."

She poked him in the chest. "Mine? It was all you, Max Radcliff."

"Nope, I was the innocent bystander," he joked.

"The main problem I can see is, no coffee."

"Oh damn, did you have to mention that, now it's all I'll think about."

"Just sharing the wealth, if I have to suffer, so do you."

"I'll bet there is coffee in those cupboards."

"Eww, I don't know how long it stays good, but I'm thinking over ten years is pushing it."

"I don't know, I might be willing to risk it." He rubbed a hand over his beard. "Of course, we don't know if we can get clean water out of the sink, or if by attempting it we might cause some kind of water disaster."

"Do you think using the toilet will cause a mess?" She could really use a potty break.

Max shrugged. "Flushing a time or two is a big step from running water until it becomes clear."

"I think I'm going to chance it." She gathered up the wet wipes, trash bag and her clothes and hurried to the bathroom. She wished she could soak in the giant claw-foot tub, but not in rusty water. She got as clean as she could, using the wet wipes, and put on her clothes from yesterday, wishing she had clean underwear.

Max sighed dramatically when she reappeared. "What a shame to cover up all that loveliness."

She rolled her eyes and handed him the wet wipes, "Your turn."

When Max had taken his clothes into the bathroom, she pulled their sheets off the lounger, folded them neatly, put them in another trash bag, and stuffed them under all their house hunting supplies. She didn't need any comments from her kids about soiled sheets.

When that was done, she smoothed the daybed, so it looked as pristine as when they'd come in the room. She decided the dust covers were too dirty to put back on. Carol would want to wash them too, but later, once everything had been assessed, and work had begun. It was no longer in doubt that she would want to do the job, it was too fine a house and remarkably sound, to abandon it.

Plus, all those books. It would take a long time just to list all of them. Unless they had left her a list in the safe deposit box. Now wouldn't that be a miracle?

Max cleaned himself up, glad the woman had brought a huge container of wet wipes. At least he wouldn't stink when they were rescued. Max dressed and hoped like hell them flushing the toilet didn't cause a shitload of trouble. Carol needed to get a plumber and electrician out here immediately. Yesterday would be good. He understood her reluctance to pull the men off the church, but at the same time she really needed their attention.

When he went back into the main room, she'd straightened it all up and had food out for them to eat. It wasn't as much as he would like, but if she'd saved some back for later in the day that was probably wise. He was certainly leaning toward not needing it. But they couldn't count on anything.

He sat in the chair next to the table with their breakfast and took a slug from the water bottle. "After we eat, we should probably start watching the gates. If you want to start, I'll carry everything down in anticipation of us getting out of here."

"But…"

He took her hand and kissed her fingers. "If they don't find us, I'll bring it all back up. I'm choosing to believe they will find us before lunch."

"All right, then I will choose to believe it also. I'll be happy to watch the gates, while you play pack mule."

They didn't talk much as they ate their meager breakfast, both of them lost in their own thoughts. When they were finished, they put their trash in the bag. Carol drifted over to the window to stand watch and he wondered if she was feeling as confident as she looked, or if it was all a brave front. Since he couldn't exactly answer that for himself, he didn't ask.

He gathered up as much as he could carry and set off down the stairs, hoping all the stairs and lovemaking hadn't hurt Carol's hip. But she'd not mentioned it, so he assumed she was fine. On the way down the stairs he marveled anew, at the way the builders had managed to project the light down four stories so efficiently. The designer of this place had been very clever, too bad his grandson was such a loser.

He'd just set the supplies on the table when she shrieked. "They're here! They're already here!"

Well, that was extremely efficient, of all of them. He looked up and couldn't see her, so she must still be by the window.

Her voice drifted down to him. "I'm going to watch until they get inside."

He went over to the door to stand as close as he could, he planned to yell if he heard the smallest peep.

He heard her start down the stairs bringing the cooler with her. He'd left the water up there, since he couldn't quite haul everything in one load. He heard her let out a yell and he rushed back into the middle. He raised his voice. "Careful on your hip, we don't want to have to go to the clinic first thing."

"Right, first thing is coffee. I'll slow down, get back over to the door."

He grinned at her bossiness and hustled back to the bookshelf. He heard a faint noise and yelled out. "Hello?"

Nothing. He listened carefully, but did not hear a peep. He waited a few minutes and yelled out again. "Hello?"

Carol joined him at the door, a little out of breath. He frowned at the speed she'd come down the steps. They both listened, hoping to hear something, anything. But all they heard was silence.

He called out again, "Hello?"

Carol echoed him. "Hello? Nolan, Terry, anyone."

They heard a scuffle and then, "Mom? Where are you?"

She beamed, and they both yelled out, "In the library."

She heard the female voice call out. "They're in the library. Come quick."

"Where in the library? The room is empty."

Max yelled out, "By the paintings."

Carol followed suit, "Behind the bookshelf."

They heard other people talking. The female was shushing all of them. "I can't hear them over all of you, now hush."

The cacophony of voices quieted. The female, Sandy maybe, called out. "Which paintings, there are paintings all over the place."

"The hanging ones." Max called out in frustration.

He heard a male say, "Wait, look there's a golden thread. I think it's pointing to that bookshelf."

"Yes, it moves." Carol called out in a shrieking tone that Max was certain had shredded his eardrum.

He yelled, "Move the furniture in front of the bookshelf."

He heard one of the guys call out. "We need to drag that desk away from the bookshelf."

As soon as they heard a dragging sound Max started pulling the shelves back along the track.

"Oh, it's folding outward, push the desk further out. Hurry," the female voice said.

There was more scraping, and the bookcase opened a little further. Far enough for a head to pop through the opening. He'd never seen this woman before, so, not Sandy. "Mom, Mr. Radcliff, we found you."

Then the head disappeared, and he heard her shriek, "Get that God damned desk out of the way."

"We are, Janet. If you will calm down and move, we need to push it toward you, there is too much crap over here?"

"Fine, but hurry the hell up."

Carol looked up at him with a smile. "My kids. Aren't they great?"

And then she burst into tears. The stoic woman who had managed just fine, the whole time they were trapped, dissolved into a blubbering mess in his arms.

CHAPTER TWENTY-NINE

*M*ax held the sobbing Carol, as her kids pushed the desk to the other side of the room and pulled the bookcase open all the way. When they rushed in surrounding her, she sniffed, rubbed the tears off her face, and turned to greet them.

"You did good, what time is it?"

Terry said, "About seven thirty."

"Did anyone bring coffee?"

Sandy laughed. "Mom. That's the first words out of your mouth? What happened?"

Carol put her hands on her hips. "It's seven thirty, normally I've had half a pot by now. As soon as I have coffee in my hands, I'll tell you all about it. Did you tell Judy to hand out coupons for breakfast?"

"Yes, and she said she could stay this morning until you get back."

Terry said, "I was up early and have nearly a whole pot at my house. I'm sure I didn't remember to turn it off. Let's go there and we can talk."

"Perfect. It's closest anyway. Can you kids take our

supplies with you?" She turned to Nolan. "Max and I will ride with you, so you can get an APB out."

Max felt like laughing at the expressions from everyone assembled when she mentioned an All-Points Bulletin, but Carol just made a shooing motion with her hands and said, "Coffee."

After they climbed into the patrol car, Carol turned serious and started spouting off information. "Joseph James Jenkinson used to work at the Legal Eagle courier. He has a handgun and is quite unstable. He alleged he had killed one of the other couriers, so he could take this job."

Max was shocked when she gave a very accurate description of the man and even knew his courier ID number. Max didn't need to say a word, he was amazed at not only her observation skills, but also her memory. He didn't know or remember half of what she told Nolan.

By the time she'd given Nolan all the details, they had pulled up to Terry's house. Max saw there was a medium-sized house on one side and a huge barn like structure on the other. Carol had mentioned that Terry built furniture, so Max assumed the barn was his workspace. Someday he would love to go look around, but not today. Today he wanted to get the inquisition over with, drink a pot or two of coffee, then go back to Carol's to shower, and hopefully eat a plateful of food at some point.

Nolan said, "I'm going to call this in. Don't get to the part about yesterday, until I get in there. You can tell your kids the story up until you brought me out to the house, but stop there if I'm not in the house by then."

Max took her hand when they had exited the police chief's vehicle. "You can introduce me to everyone, too. There was at least one person I don't know."

"Janet, yes, and it doesn't hurt to remind everyone who you are again."

He followed Carol into the house and straight back to the kitchen where every single one of them was engaged in preparing food. He wanted to weep with gratitude, or maybe cheer, instead he accepted a large cup of coffee from Terry, as did Carol.

Terry asked, "Do you take anything in it?"

"Black is just fine. Thanks."

Terry motioned over his shoulder. "They decided you might be hungry, and so are the rest of us. Thank God, I have food in the house, or they might have strung me up by my thumbs. I just got it yesterday, so I'm glad your misadventure didn't happen before it got here, or we would be having ramen noodles."

Max chuckled at Terry's mock-terrified expression. "I've been there a few times myself. Comes with the artist temperament. But I'm not going to complain that you have bacon and eggs. You'll have to get new ones after feeding this crew."

Terry shrugged. "Or go back to the ramen."

Max grinned and high-fived Terry. Carol had swept right into the kitchen and was helping get breakfast on. Max watched the commotion. Greg was making a mountain of buttered toast. Sandy was scrambling at least a dozen eggs. Janet was frying the whole pound of bacon. Carol was making a fresh pot of coffee, since Terry's first pot was drained.

Carol called out. "Terry, set the table."

Terry rolled his eyes. "Yes, Mother."

Max asked, "What can I do?"

"See if Terry has any juice in the fridge. And check for jam." She glanced around. "Other than that, I think we're good."

When everyone was seated and the food passed around,

Janet spoke up. "I know we don't do it often, but considering the circumstances, can I say a quick prayer?"

Everyone nodded and bowed their heads.

Janet spoke clearly with only a tiny waiver in her words. "Thank you, Lord, for helping us to find Mom and Max quickly, and that they were safe and not harmed. And help the police to find whoever it was that locked them in there, and get him behind bars."

Nolan said, "Amen," and slid into the last vacant spot at the table.

Carol looked around at her family and felt tears clog her throat. She was so glad to be having breakfast with them. She and Max were safe and sound. Janet was finally away from her abusive husband. Sandy had come back to their home-town and married Greg. Terry was even home early from his furniture deliveries. She had a lot to be thankful for.

Max must have noticed her not eating. He took her hand under the table and squeezed it. She looked at him in grati-tude and her throat cleared enough to swallow.

They all ate, but as they did, she saw several of them sneaking covert glances at Max, curiosity was running rampant. Might as well get it over with.

Carol put down her fork and took a long drink of coffee. Then she took the bull by the horns and spoke. "Most of you have met Max, and you all know he's in Chedwick to help finalize the plans for the church. Janet, I don't think you've met him. Max this is my middle child, Janet. Max has been helping me investigate the old Zimmerman house to see if it is feasible to make into a library for the town. He's the one that discovered that the dimensions inside the house didn't match up with the outside."

Max said, "So we've been uncovering the clues to open the secret room. We also discovered a couple of days ago that there was another person trying to find the hidden area."

Carol took back up the story. "We called in Nolan to investigate before we obscured the evidence with our tramping around. The Zimmermans left a secret message in the letter that gave us hints to the clues, and let us know about the other person."

"What we found was a library, what the other guy thought there was going to be was a treasure room," Max told the group.

Sandy said, "But books *are* treasures."

Carol beamed at her daughter. "Of course, they are, but the other guy wanted fast cash, not a bunch of musty old books."

Sandy crossed her arms over her chest and frowned. "Then he is a fool."

Max chuckled and muttered, "In more ways than one."

Carol elbowed him affectionately. "Max is right. He walked right in waiving a gun around declaring he was Joseph James Jenkinson and he had been waiting all his life to collect this treasure. He'd even pursued his career as a legal courier just to get his hands on the Zimmerman inheritance documents. His grandfather had been the original architect and had talked about all his clever inventions. So, Triple-J was obsessed."

Greg shook his head. "What a dumbass."

Max said, "True enough. His grandfather on the other hand was brilliant."

The conversation dwelled around the clever inventions for a few minutes, before Nolan reigned them in. "Please continue with the chain of events."

Carol and Max took turns relaying all that had happened, until everyone was satisfied, including Nolan.

Nolan called into dispatch to have one of his officers go out to the landing to see if Carol's vehicle was there, and if the keys were in it. By the time the officer radioed back that yes indeed it was there, with the keys in the console, everyone had finished eating.

Max asked Carol, "Do you want me to ride with Nolan to get your car? That way you could spend a few minutes with your family."

Greg walked over. "I'll go with him to make sure he can find his way back."

Max nodded. "That would be great. It did seem a little twisty."

Carol agreed with that plan. "Yes, that would be nice. I'll help the kids clean up here and then we can go back to my place for showers and clean clothes. I am rather tired of these."

"Right there with you, sweetheart."

Carol noticed a look pass between Terry and Greg, and wondered if Max would be getting the third degree from the trained attorney, who ran the local bar, and had married her daughter.

When the two men had left with Nolan, her children stopped what they were doing and surrounded her. First there were hugs and a few tears and then the inquisition started.

Surprisingly, Janet started it. "Mom, just what is going on between you and this Max person?"

"He's helping me with the Zimmerman place."

Sandy rolled her eyes. "And…."

"And it's none of your business. I, am a grown woman."

"Mom, are you sleeping with him?" Janet asked.

Terry said, "I don't think I want to hear the answer to that question. Girls, leave Mom alone."

Janet rounded on him. "You've never heard of sex, Terry?"

"Of course, I have, but I don't want to think about it in conjunction with my mother."

Sandy rolled her eyes again. "So, you think you were found under a cabbage leaf?"

"No, but that was a long time ago and with our dad. This... this is... different."

"Which is why we are asking. Mom, we don't want you to get hurt. Are you sure you know what you're doing?"

"Yes, Sandy. I am a big girl and if I have chosen to sleep with Max, not that I am saying I am, but it is my business. Your father has been gone nearly half my life and if I want to have a... a fling, I will. Now, let's clean up this kitchen."

Janet persevered, "But, Mom..."

Carol was shocked that Janet, of all people, was pressing. Janet had lied and hidden the abuse she'd taken from her ex-husband for over ten years. How dare she... wait, that was probably exactly *why* she was pushing, Janet had finally realized what all that silence had cost her and the kids. She sighed internally knowing Janet wouldn't push if she didn't love her. But she needed to stop this discussion now.

Carol said firmly, but not angrily, "Janet, drop it."

Sandy said, "We just don't want to see you get hurt, Mom."

"I'll be fine, now let's get this kitchen cleaned up. I need to go back and see how my guests, and Judy, faired in my absence."

They cleaned up in relative silence, which gave Carol time to wonder about sleeping with Max. Was it just a fling, like she'd told the kids? She didn't exactly like the sound of that. But it couldn't really be anything more. He lived and worked in the city, and she ran her bed and breakfast here. She'd tried not to think about that. Carol enjoyed Max's company too much. Was she going to end up heartbroken?

CHAPTER THIRTY

*N*olan said, "Give me a few minutes with the SUV. Just to see if I can raise some evidence to support the eyewitness account. You guys can just wait in the cruiser."

When Nolan had shut the door, Greg turned toward Max. "So, just what are your intentions with my mother-in-law?"

Max was startled at the question. It wasn't like he was a teenager out to ruin the woman. She was in her fifties and was a widow. "My intentions are to help her explore options for renovating the Zimmerman house into a library. She's hired me, or our firm, to do some designs for her. Starting with the first floor. We've worked on several ideas."

Greg nodded. "That's great, but you and I both know that's not what I was asking."

Max looked the other man in the eye. "My relationship with Carol is my business and hers, and no one else's. We are both in our fifties, we are both widowed, and we both know what we're doing."

"All right, but you must also understand that we're concerned that when you leave, she will be hurt by that. She's a strong woman and ran this city single handedly for years. Terry's dad died when he was just a kid, so she's been widowed for nearly half her life, which means she might be a little more vulnerable than you are. We just don't want to see her hurt when you go back to your life."

Max ran a hand down his beard as he thought about what the younger man had said. "I'll keep that in mind. I don't have any desire to hurt her, Greg. She's a mighty fine woman."

"Good enough."

Max let Greg drive rather than being the navigator. He knew the roads and had probably driven Carol's car before, plus it gave Max time to think about the other man's words. Was he going to hurt Carol when he left? It wasn't like he'd hidden the fact that he would be leaving, once he was no longer needed. Carol knew that. So, there would be no surprises.

He knew he would miss her like crazy when they went their separate ways. She might feel the same way, here in a place where she had been the authority figure for too long to be able to be a woman. Max knew that was a lot of the reason she hadn't ever had a lover after her husband had died.

What about his own feelings? She had opened his heart back up. He'd hardly noticed the anniversary of his wife's death. He knew he would always love Jeanette, and he would always miss her, but Carol had filled a hole in him that had been an aching chasm. He wasn't sure what would happen when he got back to the city and his solitary life. Sure, he had his brother and friends, but not a soft caring presence like Carol was. She was also his perfect match in bed. Damn, it was going to suck when he left.

Did he really want to leave? The idea niggled but he pushed it down, he had to, his life was in the city. His brother, his business, his home, they were all in the city. But not Carol... No, he needed to stop these foolish thoughts right now.

He could always go visit his brother. He could work remotely. He could keep his house in the city for occasional visits. Or rent it out. Or sell it. No, this was foolish thinking, he needed to get a grip.

Maybe he should taper off his relationship with Carol, before either of them got more involved. Now that they had found the hidden room, he could just go home. He wasn't needed at the church anymore. Carol had several of his suggestions for ways to refurbish the house. The next step would be to get a plumber and electrician in there to assess the place. Then a cleaning crew. She didn't really need him right now either.

He should go home, but why did that idea cause so much pain in his chest? Rather than the pain changing his mind, it made him realize he'd already stayed too long. If he wanted to get out of this unscathed, he needed to go, now.

Max was so damn glad when they pulled up to Terry's house again, so he had something else to think about. Greg helped him load all their supplies into the back of Carol's car. Max hoped they didn't need to stay much longer, he wanted a shower in the worst way.

After he'd gotten that, he would pack up his stuff and tell Carol he was leaving. It was the only way.

Carol could tell something had changed the minute Max walked back into Terry's house. He was friendly enough, explaining that it had taken them a while so Nolan could check for evidence. But the comradery, or intimacy, between them had vanished. She looked at Greg and he didn't give any indication of anything, but she'd seen the look he'd exchanged with Terry before he'd left, and she just knew he was behind the change in Max.

Dammit, her kids had bombarded her, and Greg had obviously said something to Max, and Max had taken it to heart. Damn, damn, damn.

Max asked, "Are you ready to go?"

"Yes." She held out her hand to him, but he pretended like he didn't see it, while he said goodbye to her kids. This was not going to be good. He'd already pulled away in the short time he'd been gone. She wanted to kick Greg and maybe her kids too, but she just said her goodbyes and walked silently to the car.

Max tried to make small talk as she drove, but she wasn't listening. She was trying to figure out if she could restore her closeness to Max or if she should just let it go. Carol didn't want to let it go, she wanted more time with him, more closeness, more sex. But only if the three went hand in hand.

When she didn't respond to his small talk he gave up and they spent the rest of the drive in quiet, they'd spent a lot of time together not talking, but this time it wasn't a comfortable silence, like the others had been. Carol thought about asking him what he was thinking, but decided she needed to check in with Judy and see to any remaining guests, before she opened that can of worms. She was certain the discussion was going to be unpleasant.

When they got to the inn, they gathered up their supplies to carry them into the house. They put them down and Max muttered something about a shower, just as Judy swooped in asking questions while she hugged Carol with a bone-breaking strength.

Carol gave Judy the shortened version and asked about the guests. Only one person had moaned about having to go out for breakfast, and that was a cranky old man that wasted more food than he ate, and was leaving tomorrow.

"Can you stay a few more minutes while I jump in the shower and get some clean clothes? I'm not a fan of wearing the same clothes two days in a row."

"Eww, I know how you feel. Sure, I can stay until you're ready."

"Thanks. It will only take a few minutes."

Judy hugged her again, no less bone crushing than the first. "I'm just so glad you are all right, when I got here this morning, I was so scared."

Carol wrenched herself free and took a step back. "I'm glad you were here, so you could sound the alarm. We were comfortable, but it was still stressful. I'll be down in a jiffy."

Carol hurried to her room. She and Judy had never hugged before, they didn't have that kind of relationship, but she supposed stress changed things. Sometimes for the good, and sometimes for the bad. But life went on, and she would too.

CHAPTER THIRTY-ONE

*M*ax fought a battle with himself, even as he gathered up his clothes and computer and drawing supplies. The idea of leaving filled him with dread, even as the thoughts of staying equally tantalized and scared the crap out of him. He couldn't lose any more of his heart to her, leaving was the only option.

He flipped open his sketch pad and found the drawing he'd done of Carol. It seemed almost flat, now that he knew her so much better, lifeless. He'd captured her looks and a tiny portion of her essence, but it was nothing like he would draw now. There were so many facets of her that were missing. Maybe it was impossible to capture everything about the fascinating woman.

He closed the sketchpad and put it in his computer bag. A knock sounded on the door and he knew it would be Carol. He didn't feel ready to see her, but if he was going to be on the ferry this afternoon, he needed to talk to her. He sucked it up and opened the door.

"Come in," he said roughly.

She came in and her eyes zeroed in immediately to his

bed, where his suitcase was open and nearly full. "You're leaving."

It wasn't a question, but he answered anyway. "Yes, we found the secret room, I've already drawn up several sets of plans for renovation. You and the contractor can decide which ones to use. The church project doesn't need me any longer. I don't see any reason to stay."

She winced, and he realized he'd phrased that poorly. He tried again, "I've enjoyed our time together. You are a spectacular woman and any man would be lucky to be with you, but we both knew this was temporary and I would be leaving."

"Yes, we did, but I thought there might be a little more closure on it rather than you packing your bags and walking out. Maybe a more gradual transition."

"I don't think I can do gradual." He didn't know what else to say. He couldn't just blurt everything out. No, it was better this way, fast and final. "I'm sorry, I just have to go. Thank you so much. If you need anything on the designs, please feel free to contact me."

"Fine, have a nice trip home, I will put the charges on your card. Please invoice me for your architect services." Carol said in a voice so icy, he was sure to get frostbite, then she turned and strode out of the door her head held high.

Max felt like the best thing in his life had just walked out the door. But he could not think of a damn thing he could do that wouldn't make matters worse.

Carol marched down the stairs in a fury. Call him if she needed anything with the designs? Unless hell froze over, there was no way she was going to talk to him again. He wanted a fast breakup, well he was going to get it. Jerk.

When she got downstairs, she grabbed her purse and car keys. There was no way she was staying until he left, and he could walk to the landing. She was going to go talk to the librarian about some ideas. Max would never find her there, she could park behind the building. After the ferry left, she would go by the church and see when the electrician and plumber would be available. She would keep herself busy until the damn ferry, with asshole Max, was long gone. Then she could go home, lock herself in her room with a bottle of wine and cry her eyes out.

Knowing something was going to happen, and having it actually occur, were two entirely different things. She might have to have a chat with Greg and her kids. Nosy busybodies. She just knew Greg had started this instantaneous flight. Not that she was going to blame it all on the kids, Max should have been a man and stood up to them.

But she didn't want them meddling in her life. If she found someone else, she was not about to let them scare him off. Carol sighed, it had taken over twenty years to meet Max, she would be in her seventies if it took that long again.

Carol wanted to kick something, instead she drove through town... her town. She'd loved it her whole life, but it seemed a little colorless at the moment. Damn man.

She parked behind the library and went in, since it was summer, the librarian had some high school students working. One was reading a children's book to a handful of early grade school students, while their mothers milled around among the shelves, or sat and listened.

Carol didn't' see her grandkids in attendance, but since Janet had been out looking for her and that man, she wasn't sure what she'd done with them. She knew Janet did bring them to story time in the summer, it was a few moments for parents to have some down time.

Another high school student was manning the checkout

desk. Carol could see the librarian, Patty Anne, in the back-room processing books. Her long dark hair was pulled back from her face, cascading down her back in tight curls, and her glasses rode on the tip of her nose. Carol waited for a moment trying to catch Patty Anne's eye. It didn't take long for her to look up and see Carol watching her. She waived her into the room.

"To what do I owe the pleasure of your company?"

Carol smiled. "You know that you're always bemoaning how small this building is, and that you have to share it with the hair salon? Which can get stinky."

Patty Anne nodded.

"Well, have I got a story for you."

"Really? Let's go to my office slash break room and talk about it. The girls have the front covered and they know where to find me."

An hour and a half later, Carol walked out of the library in a much better mood and Patty Anne was floating on air.

After that she went by the church and got both an electrician and a plumber scheduled. They would be there this week, so she would know so much more, about how soon she could get busy on the house. After those two were finished with their assessment and work, she would need a cleaning crew, and then Patty Anne and she could start cataloging the books.

If she kept busy, she could keep her mind off Max. The nights were going to be hell though. She sighed and decided to go to Amber's for food. She hadn't eaten since Terry's house this morning, she wasn't particularly hungry, but she needed to eat something, and it was past the lunch rush, so maybe she could get Amber to keep her company.

When Carol walked into the mostly empty restaurant Amber looked up from her paperwork and waived. She kept watching the door for a moment and then walked over to where Carol stood. "Where's Max?" the younger woman asked.

"Halfway to Chelan. He's on his way home."

Amber looked at her for a long moment and said, "Is he coming back?"

"No, he is not." Carol had to fight the tears that threatened.

Amber picked up a menu and ushered Carol over to a table and sat down with her.

Thank God the woman simply sat in silence with her as she tried to look over the menu and get her composure back. But she couldn't see a thing. Finally, she put it down and asked, "What kind of soup do you have today?"

"Clam chowder and tomato bisque."

A waitress walked up. "I'll have a bowl of tomato bisque and an iced tea."

"Bring me an iced tea too, please," Amber said.

When the waitress had left, Amber asked, "Do you want to talk about it?"

She did want to talk about it, but she also did not want to start blubbering. So, no talking about it. "No. But I do have kind of an interesting story to tell."

Carol ate her soup while she told Amber all about the Zimmerman house. She was almost finished with her tale when her mouth got away from her. "He just packed his bags and left. When we got locked in the library the kids had to come rescue us and we went to Terry's house for breakfast, because I wasn't ready to face people at the inn, and Judy was there. Max and Greg went to the landing to get my car. My kids tried to stage an intervention and I told them to back off. I think Greg said something to Max, and he caved."

Amber took her hand but didn't offer up any stupid platitudes, for which Carol was grateful.

"I knew he wasn't going to stay forever, but I thought it

would be a gradual thing. That he would hang around a while longer, to see about the plumbing and electrical. But no, it was just, we found the room so I'm leaving." Tears threatened, so she stopped talking and pushed her spoon around in her bowl.

Amber said softly, "I'm so sorry, Carol. Men can be such idiots sometimes."

Carol laughed, but it had both a bitter and a watery sound to it. She cleared her throat. "I'll get out of your hair, you probably have a million things to do."

"Don't you worry about that, I have staff, and friendship is more important than commerce."

"True, but I've been neglecting my commerce, so I need to get back to it. Thanks for keeping me company."

CHAPTER THIRTY-TWO

*M*ax walked into his empty house, still trying to convince himself he'd done the right thing by leaving Chedwick. He'd listed every reason, over and over again on the slow ferry ride, and then again on the long drive back to the city. But it wasn't helping. Before he did something stupid, like getting back in his car and driving straight back to Chedwick, he called his brother.

"Hey Max, howzit going?"

"I'm back."

"Back? Why?"

"What do you mean why? I live here."

"Well yeah, but I thought you might have changed your mind." Max could almost feel his brother shrug. "You seemed pretty happy hanging out with Carol."

"She's a wonderful woman, but not for me," Max said gruffly.

"I don't see why not. You two hit it off pretty quickly. You don't have to be in the city to work, you could pack up your desktop computer and take it with you and work remotely."

"But…"

"We could teleconference if we needed to talk face to face. Or you could come back once a month for a few days if needed. It's not that far."

"But… my house."

"What about it, you don't really live there. It's hardly got any furniture in it. A couple of chairs, a TV and a bed. Is there even any food in your refrigerator?"

Max knew it was bare of food, other than a couple of frozen meals and condiments. So, he ignored the question, which Wes didn't seem to notice as he plowed on.

"You sold the old house so it wouldn't remind you of Jeanette. I get that, but you didn't make the new house a home either. You've just been walking through the days like some kind of zombie."

Max huffed and started to complain, but Wes just talked right over him. "But then you went to Chelan and things changed. Your voice had life in it again. You were intrigued by the renovation, something you normally detest. You sounded like the old Max. If all you're going to do is go back to zombie Max, I want no part of it."

"But…"

"But nothing, come into the office tomorrow, and we can talk about it. In the meantime, think about what I said, or start packing, whichever floats your boat."

Max pushed end, and flopped into his chair. Well, hell.

He looked around his living room. There were two chairs and a TV. Between the two chairs was a folding table for drinks and the remote, it had one beer bottle on it. There was a pair of dirty socks by his chair. There were no pictures on the wall. No rug on the hard wood floor, not even a book or magazine.

He walked to the kitchen. There was no table in the dining room, or even in the kitchen. He ate most of his meals standing over the sink, or at the bar, which had two barstools. He opened the cupboards, he'd not brought a single thing from his old house. Not even plates, he'd bought everything new. Which meant he'd gone to a discount store and bought a set of dishes, four plates, four bowls, four cups, and four saucers, plain white. There were eight glasses and eight sets of utensils. The refrigerator had condiments and a few frozen meals, just like he'd thought.

He padded down the hall to his bedroom. There was a bed with two pillows, a nightstand, that did have a book on it. Yay for him. And the phone charger. His closet was full, and so was a little plastic set of drawers he'd picked up to keep underclothes in. God, he really was pathetic.

The spare room he used as an office did have a decent desk and chair. There was nothing on the desk. Not even a notepad or a pen. He'd had more of his stuff out on the desk in his rented room at Carol's than he did in his own house. Just what in the hell did that mean?

Was Wes right? Did he just shuffle through the days like a zombie?

Carol was thrilled with the results of the inspections. The plumber had declared that the water system was in good condition, due to the upgrade in the bathroom above the library. Adding the shower had caused the Zimmermans to upgrade all the pipes, he said they had done that just a couple of years before they had left town.

The electrician had echoed the claims that there had been renovations done to the electrical system in the last twenty years, and since the building was surprisingly free from rodents, she should be able to use the wiring currently in place, providing they didn't install a bunch of air-conditioning or other major appliances. He'd said for their cleaning and investigation of the library room they should be fine.

They made a plan to do some more upgrading, because she wasn't completely sure she wouldn't want air in the summer months. It could get plenty hot in their part of the world. Although the stone building did seem to hold off some of the heat. But better safe than sorry.

The best part of that news was that she and Patty Anne were itching to start their inventory of the old books. And Carol knew having Patty Anne in the building would erase the memories of Max. Carol needed that to happen as soon as humanly possible, she was tired of being sad and grumpy. He'd only been gone a week, but it had seemed like an eternity to Carol.

As soon as she had the all clear she quickly dialed Patty Anne's number. The other woman answered on the first ring. She didn't even say hello. "What did they say?"

"We're clear to go. The plumbing is fine, the electricity is adequate for our needs, we can start anytime."

Patty Anne's screech nearly blew out Carol's eardrums. "Oh my God, can we go now?"

"It's getting kind of late."

"Late for what. If we can turn on the lights I am totally there."

"Dinner time?"

"I'll grab something from Amber's on my way to your house. Please? I've been dreaming about this for a week."

Carol laughed. "All right you've convinced me. Just honk when you get here, and I'll come out."

"Goody, goody, goody. I may pass out from excitement."

"If you do that you'll fall down, and have to go to the clinic, and we won't get there at all."

"You're right. No passing out. I'll be there in fifteen minutes."

Carol just laughed. She'd planned to have a cleaning crew start on the place before they started looking at the books, but Patty Anne had called her every day to ask about the progress, insisting that she couldn't care less about dust and spiders.

Carol went upstairs to change into jeans, a long-sleeved t-shirt, and some sneakers. As she walked back down the stairs, she heard a horn honk. Patty Anne had arrived. Carol grabbed her bag of supplies and walked out to Patty Anne's car, the woman was vibrating with excitement.

Bouncing up and down in the driver's seat, Patty Anne said, "I can't wait to get my hands on those books. I brought a tablet to keep track of the details, and paper in case the battery dies, or something horrible happens."

Carol laughed and shook her head, she'd never seen anyone quite so excited about a bunch of dusty books. While giving Patty Anne directions to the house, Carol thought about the enormous number of tomes in the library, and wondered how long it would take to just make a list.

She should probably give Patty Anne a key, so she could work whenever she was able. Carol didn't have the time to be here much, except for in the afternoon and some evenings. She thought Patty Anne might want to spend a lot more time than Carol could. In fact, she might want to move in, there was plenty of space. Something to think about.

When they got in the gate and close enough to see the house Patty Anne slammed on the brakes and gasped. Staring out the window she said, "It's enormous, that's way bigger than we need for a library, what are we going to do with all of it?"

Carol shrugged. "I have no idea, really. The first floor would be a processing room, break room, and the rest as a library. The second floor could be an office for you and maybe meeting rooms. Third floor? No idea. The tower in the middle is all library right now except for the fourth floor which is half library, half living space. I brought some copies of some ideas for renovating the first floor."

Carol had forced herself to print out Max's drawings. She was determined to move past his leaving, so she had to be an adult about the plans he'd drawn up. But it had taken a toll on her heart to see them again.

Patty Anne started forward until she pulled into the parking area. "We'll need more parking."

"Good point." Carol hadn't thought much about the outside area, other than getting it cleaned up, but Patty Anne was right, they would need more parking. A fresh set of eyes would give her a new perspective.

They went right in and didn't dawdle but went straight to the library.

Patty Anne said, "Oh are we going to start in this room?"

"No. Follow me." Carol went to the bookcase that hid the secret door and pushed it open.

Patty Anne clapped her hands. "That is awesome."

"Not as awesome as what's behind it."

Carol led the way so she could watch Patty Anne's reaction. It was all she'd hoped for. Even though she'd told the woman all about the hidden, four-story library, the shock of seeing it for the first time was priceless.

Patty Anne managed to walk into the center of the room before she froze, her eyes looking up and up and up, her mouth hanging open farther and farther as she looked higher and higher. Finally, she looked at Carol, shook her head and whispered. "I know you tried to warn me, but I had no idea. It's incredible, and there are books all the way to the fourth floor?"

"Not just books all the way up, but every floor is packed full. It's going to take weeks, months maybe, just to write down the title, author name, and publishing date. Yes, unless you bring in more help."

"I need to think about this," Patty Anne said with a bewildered expression.

The doorbell chimed with a kind of dull clunk. "You think. while I go answer the door. I don't know who it could be."

Patty Anne didn't answer, she had the faraway look in her eyes of someone thinking hard.

There was a strange man at the door. Behind him was a semi-truck, no two trucks. "May I help you?"

"Carol Anderson?"

"Yes."

"Sign here."

"What am I signing for?" she asked.

The two pods, sent from Phoenix, Arizona."

There were no pods, just two semi-trucks. Were the pods inside? "But... I don't see any pods."

The man frowned. "The trailer *is* the pod."

Carol nearly screeched, he had to be joking. "What. The whole trailer? Two of them?"

"Yes ma'am, where do you want them?"

"I have no idea. There isn't room out here in front. Let's look in back."

The two of them walked to the rear of the house. There was a flat area where they might fit. The man pulled off his baseball cap and scratched his nearly bald head. "That will have to do. It will take some maneuvering to get them both into it, but I think we can manage."

Carol's head was swimming at the idea of both those trailers full of books. She tried to stay calm as she asked the man, "Are the trailers full?"

"Oh yeah, both of us have a couple of boxes in our front seats to get them all here."

Carol didn't know whether to laugh or cry. "Great. Can you leave the boxes on the porch?"

"We're not supposed to carry or unload things, but we can put them on the porch for you without anyone knowing."

Carol managed one word. "Thanks."

"You can go on inside if you like, we'll bring the boxes up last and ring the bell to let you know we're finished."

She nodded and went back into the house. She looked in her purse and found two twenties she could tip the men with. Then she went back into the library to tell Patty Anne more books had arrived.

A little while later when the doorbell clunked again, Carol went to the door, to find the two drivers on her porch, next to an enormous stack of boxes. There was no way she was going to get those in the house by herself. She'd have to get Terry and Greg to move them. She gave each man a twenty and thanked them for putting the boxes on the porch. Shaking her head, she walked back to the library where she and Patty Anne had barely gotten through one shelf. There were more books than that on the porch.

She went back to join Patty Anne and decided not to mention the gigantic stack of boxes on the porch. Focusing on the task at hand she reached for another book, she'd barely finished typing the information into her own tablet when the doorbell clunked again. Wondering what the truck drivers needed now, she wiped her dirty hands on her jeans, and pushed back a lock of hair that kept getting in her eyes, as she walked back to the front door and pulled it open.

"Max."

CHAPTER THIRTY-THREE

*M*ax had never seen anything so beautiful than the woman who answered the sickly doorbell. She had on jeans that were filthy, her shirt was covered in dust, and there was a smear of grime on her forehead. But under all the dirt was a beautiful woman, whose eyes were spitting fire. There had been one quick moment of joy, before the anger roared into place and her eyes turned furious. There was probably some pain hiding in there somewhere, but anger was winning over all other emotions.

"What are you doing here?"

He opened his mouth, but she held up a hand stopping him. "No. I don't want to know. I don't care. I don't want to have anything to do with you. Get off my land."

"Carol."

"No, go away, Max. I'm not interested in anything you have to say."

Shit, she was mad as hell. He'd never once considered that. Her anger was magnificent. Her eyes flashed and color flooded her face. She was so damn beautiful, and pissed, oh so pissed. He gestured to the right. "I could get the boxes in off the porch."

She narrowed her eyes at him, then looked at the tower of boxes. "Fine, you can bring the boxes in and then you're leaving."

He nodded and turned to grab the first box. She stepped out of the way and he carried it inside. "Library?

She huffed. "No, it's full. Maybe the parlor."

"There are semi-trailers in the back."

"Those are the pods of books." Just thinking about those trailers made her tired.

"Are you shitting me? Those aren't pods. Are they full?"

"The boxes are filled with what wouldn't fit."

A burst of laughter escaped him. "I'm sorry. I know it's not funny, but…" Another chuckle escaped. "What were they thinking?"

A tiny smile crept over her lips. "I have no idea. It's going to take weeks to get through the books in the house. Let alone the boxes. I can't even think of the trailers."

They had gotten back to the porch and he picked up another very heavy box. By the time he hauled them all inside he was going to have to put ice on his back. But anything to keep her talking to him. He shook his head and another chuckle escaped. "With the number of books you've inherited, you might just use the second floor for stacks too."

A small whiff of laughter escaped Carol. "I know, it's like they just keep coming and coming. It's getting ridiculous."

"Multiplying like rabbits."

"Way worse than bunnies. Those at least have a gesta-tional period." She chuckled.

"And they left you money to buy more." He pointed out with a wicked smile.

Carol laughed and then groaned, "Don't remind me. Buy

ANOTHER CHANCE FOR LOVE

more? Not any time soon. I hope they didn't do anything crazy, like set up an auto order."

Max let out a belly laugh at her utterly horrified expression. "That would be a disaster, but I wouldn't put it past them."

"I may have to change my name, go into hiding." She giggled.

Max had a great idea how to change her name, but he wasn't going to mention that right now. He just kept carrying those damn heavy boxes. When he set the last one down, he wiped his forehead with his shirt sleeve. "Could I talk you out of a bottle of water?"

She frowned, but then nodded. "Yes, you earned it."

He followed her into the hidden library where another woman was working. The other woman looked up and smiled. "Hello, I'm Patty Anne, the librarian."

Max gave her a professional smile. "I'll bet you're in hog heaven then. I'm Max Radcliff, architect."

She jumped up and put the book down she was cataloging. "Oh, did you design the plans? Can I ask you about them?"

"I did." He glanced at Carol seeking her permission.

She sighed and nodded. "Of course, he can, Patty Anne. But he can't stay long."

He said innocently, "I'm in no hurry."

Carol narrowed her eyes at him, so he turned toward Patty Anne. "What did you want to ask me about?"

He spent over an hour answering the many questions Patty Anne asked him. She wanted to know every little detail. There were also a lot of suggestions, some were good ideas and others were impractical. They came up with a reasonable idea that he promised to draw up for her.

He'd come up with an idea to keep Carol from kicking him to the curb. "I could start on the books we just put in the parlor, they are bound to be more recent than these, so don't need your expertise, Patty Anne. I've got the time and feel bad for you two ladies working so hard with such a daunting task ahead of you."

He could tell Carol was going to tell him to go pound sand, but Patty Anne spoke first. "That would be awesome. The semi-trailers probably have newer books in them too. How long are you staying?"

He didn't answer that question directly. "I'm able to work remotely, so I've got time."

Patty Anne clapped her hands together, her eyes shining with enthusiasm. "Great. And I can hardly wait to see the new drawing. Isn't this terrific, Carol?"

"Terrific." Carol answered in a flat monotone that told Max she was not a happy camper.

Patty Anne either didn't notice or didn't want to acknowledge it. "We're just noting titles, author, and publishing date. Do you have a tablet?"

"I'll get started on my phone and bring my tablet tomorrow."

Carol grabbed his arm and said to Patty Anne, "I'll go get him set up and I'll be right back."

She marched him back to the parlor, he ambled along, perfectly happy to have her hand on his arm. When they got to the room, she shut the door and whirled on him. "Just what in the hell are you doing?"

"Helping catalogue the books."

"No, what are you doing back here in Chedwick?"

"I realized I didn't want to leave, so I came back."

"You've been gone over a week."

"I had something to wrap up and talk over with my brother."

She huffed and then crossed her arms over her chest.

"Well I am not taking back up with you. You had your chance and you blew it, buddy."

He had every intention of worming his way back into her good graces, into her life, and into her bed again, but now was not the time to go there, so all he said was, "I'm sorry."

She turned on her tail and marched out the door.

Carol was furious and thrilled in equal measure. Her whole being warred between the two reactions at having Max appear on her porch. The furious part of her wanted to slap the thrilled part, and the thrilled part of her wanted to lock the furious part away in a dungeon.

She had no intention of letting Max see anything but the furious. She was determined to keep him at arm's length. If he thought for one minute that she would take right back up where they had left off, he had another think coming.

The angry part agreed whole heartedly with that plan. We should at least find out why he's back, the thrilled part whispered. She could admit to being curious, but she hardened her heart and refused to give in.

She stopped dead in her tracks on the way back to the library. Where was he going to stay? She didn't want him back under her roof. She would lie and tell him her whole place was filled, that someone had called after he left, and she booked his room.

Carol called the little hotel, when the phone was answered she breathed a sigh of relief that she'd gotten the hotel manager. "Hi Marilyn, this is Carol. I was wondering if you had any vacancies."

"Let me look. Are you overbooked?"

"Kind of."

Marilyn laughed. "I see we have a room open right now for three days, but over the weekend we're booked solid."

Carol frowned, only three days. But better than nothing, she would have to think about what to do with him after that. "He'll take it, Max Radcliff."

"The architect? I thought he was staying at your place and that you two were getting kind of chummy."

Small towns, Carol wanted to sigh, but that would be too telling. "Things change, he had to leave, and I filled his room, now he's back."

"It can be crazy in our job with people coming and going. I'll put his name down for the next three nights."

"Thanks, Marilyn."

With that taken care of, with only one tiny lie, she went back to the hidden library to work with Patty Anne.

The woman looked up when Carol walked in. "If you want to work with the hunky architect, he can take my place and I can work on the boxes. I heard you two were getting cozy."

"Nope, we're just friends. Besides, I think you should be the one looking over these older books. You know how to handle them better than we do."

Patty Anne shrugged and went back to her book. Carol moved to the next one in her shelf. They worked for several hours, and Carol felt like it was time for a break, her back was hurting from sitting bent over books.

Max walked in like he'd heard her thoughts. "Do you ladies plan on working all night? I was thinking some food would be good. Do you want me to go grab something?"

Carol wanted to say no, but she was a little hungry, they'd eaten earlier, but a little dessert wouldn't go amiss, or even a cup of coffee, but mostly she needed to move.

Patty Anne pulled out her phone. "It's later than I thought it was. I think we should knock off for the day. Do you guys want to go to Amber's for a piece of pie?" She looked up just as she said that and frowned, then looked down at herself. "Oh, we're not really decent to go out in public, are we?"

Carol looked at Patty Anne covered head to toe in dust. Carol was certain she was just as bad. Max was a little dusty, but not like they were. Dammit she was going to have to take him up on his offer. "Yes, Max, go get something for dessert, I'll put a pot of coffee on. Patty Anne, do you want to go to my house where we can wash up a bit and eat whatever Max brings back?"

"Yes, please. I want to talk to you about some ideas that came into my mind while we were working."

Max took their orders for Amber's and said he would meet them at Carol's.

She didn't realize until she was almost home, that Amber might have a word or two to say to Max. First, she felt a little panicky about that idea, and then she shrugged internally, and decided he got what was coming to him.

CHAPTER THIRTY-FOUR

*M*ax needed more than dessert, he needed food. He'd not eaten much today, trying to get back to Carol as quickly as he could. He'd gotten some fast food as he drove as fast as he could back to Chelan. He'd had a sandwich on the barge as they poked along up the lake. He didn't think the barge took any longer than the ferry had, but each minute had dragged by.

He'd hoped she would be glad to see him. He'd stopped by the B&B and then gone straight to the Zimmermans, thinking maybe she was working at it. He'd been right about that, but not about her being happy to see him. Her eyes had shot fire at him, he was surprised he wasn't at least singed, from the look she'd given him.

It had been fortuitous that Patty Anne had been there, if she hadn't welcomed his help, he knew Carol wouldn't have allowed him to stay for one minute. He was completely out of his depth with Carol, he didn't know how to convince her to give him a second chance.

He walked into Amber's restaurant; Amber was the hostess. "I need to place a to go order."

Amber stared at him for a long moment and then handed him a menu. "Wait right over there."

He already knew what he wanted but he took the menu and stood to the side as instructed, while she seated several other groups that came in after him. When everyone had been dealt with, she brought a waitress over to take his order, then pulled him even further off to the side, and rounded on him with her hands on her hips.

"I thought you left."

He opened his mouth to explain, but she didn't let him. "You hurt Carol's feelings. Does she know you're back?"

"Yes, one of the—"

She cut him off again. "Of course. We don't appreciate people coming into town and toying with folks that are important to us."

"I know I—"

She narrowed her eyes at him. "So why did you come back and how long are you staying this time?"

"Are you going to let me answer?"

"I don't know. I'm pretty angry at you. You hurt one of the dearest people I know, what I really want to do is punch you in the nose."

"I was scared."

That surprised her. "Of Carol? She doesn't have a mean bone in her body."

"Not of Carol, of the way I was feeling about her."

Amber's hands dropped from her hips. "Oh."

"I started feeling things I hadn't felt since my wife died, and it scared the crap out of me, so I ran home to where it was safe. Where I could go back to my quiet life and not have to deal with all the messy emotions I was feeling."

"So…"

"My brother called me on my crap and told me he was tired of my zombie existence, and to quit being an idiot. He

201

said I'd had more life in my voice while I was here than he'd heard in years, and why in the hell was I giving that up?'

"So, I took a couple of days and really examined my life in the city. He was right, I was barely existing. I took a couple more days to decide if I was strong enough to rejoin the living. I finally came to the conclusion that I was, and that with Carol, was where I wanted to be."

"What did Carol say to that?"

"She's not exactly speaking to me, so I haven't been able to tell her. When I first showed up, she told me to get off her land. But I managed to convince her to let me carry in a mountain of heavy boxes. As soon as I get something on my stomach, I'm going to take a hand full of pain killers, so that I might be able to walk tomorrow."

Amber grinned like it served him right. This woman clearly had a mean streak.

"Patty Anne was happy to accept my help going through all the books, so then Carol was stuck."

"Sneaky."

"No, but I'll take what I can get. Please tell me how I can convince her to give me a second chance." He hated the pleading tone of his voice, but it was how he was feeling, he needed help, and since Carol had obviously confided in Amber, she might have some ideas.

"I don't know that you deserve a second chance."

"Amber, please. I want to stay and build a life with her."

She didn't say anything else, she went over to check some people out, while he waited for his food. Trying to think of a way to get Carol to at least talk to him.

When his food came out, he went up to get it and pay for it. Amber took his money, as if he were a stranger, like any other customer in her restaurant. He couldn't help the hopeless feeling that washed over him. He'd thought Amber might steer him in some direction, but it was clear she had no intention of helping him.

She handed him his change and said, "Carol's never been wooed. She and Jim played together as children, they just started there and went to dating and then got married. She's never been romanced."

"Like—"

"You'll have to figure that out, I've said enough, it's got to be from your heart, not mine."

All right, he got that. "Thank you. I appreciate it." Then he put all his change into the tip jar and walked out with his food and a lighter step. He could come up with a romance plan.

He was a little distracted while he ate dinner, letting Patty Anne and Carol's conversation roll over him, while he thought about what romancing Carol might entail. Flowers for sure, even he, knew *that* much. Chocolates, most women liked chocolates, in one of those heart shaped boxes, or was that too corny? Making her coffee in the morning before she got started cooking breakfast. He wasn't much of a morning person, but he would be for her, maybe he could help her out in the kitchen, or do any minor repairs she needed done.

When Patty Anne yawned and stood to go, Max stood also. He and Carol walked to the door and watched as Patty Anne got in her vehicle and drove off.

Carol turned to him. "I booked you a room in the hotel for the next three days. You'll need to find something for after that."

Max was astounded, she'd booked him a room? All his romance plans went up in smoke, he'd counted on staying here to woo her back. Dammit, she was not even willing to have him in her house. "Oh, well, thank you."

He walked through the still open door, this was going to be harder than he thought.

～

Carol should have felt some satisfaction at the surprise Max had shown over her booking him a room, but she just felt sad. He'd wanted to stay, and part of her had wanted him to, but she had to be strong, she wasn't cut out for a guy to flit in and out of her life. She didn't have it in her to be an on again off again lover.

Although this time he had brought his truck, and just what did that mean. He'd not brought it on the barge the first time when he'd been planning to stay for a month or more, so why did he bring it this time. Did he plan to stay even longer?

Carol had been a little surprised when Max had brought their food, not looking the least bit scathed from his encounter with Amber. In fact, he had looked happier than when he'd left. That couldn't be right, there was no way Amber wouldn't have said anything at all, unless he hadn't seen her. Oh well, she supposed she shouldn't expect other people to fight her battles, she was perfectly capable of fighting them herself.

He'd been distracted while he ate his dinner and she and Patty Anne had talked over pie. The worst part of it all was he looked so damn good in his black t-shirt, plaid shirt only partially buttoned and black jeans. God that man was a hunk, men always seemed to get better looking as they aged, while women got crow's feet and bags, it just wasn't fair.

She locked up and went to shower, she was covered head to toe in dust, all her clothes were filthy. She'd washed her hands and the dirt smudge off her face when they'd gotten back to her house, but that's all she and Patty Anne had had the strength to do. They'd put in a long day and the days weren't going to get any shorter.

If she admitted the truth, she was glad Max had come

back and was helping. Even if he only did the boxes that would be a huge advantage. Those two semi-trailers full of books had about brought her to her knees. The Zimmermans were clearly insane and had had a ton of money.

The cleaning crew would be starting tomorrow, Patty Anne was going over early to let them in, Carol had decided to have them clean the whole house, top to bottom, before she let them into the library, and the hidden area. She didn't know what to do about Max taking up the parlor to go through the boxes. Maybe they could clean around him, or maybe they could do that room first, Max wasn't much of an early morning person.

CHAPTER THIRTY-FIVE

*M*ax was up at the crack of dawn. He'd heard Carol and Patty Anne talking about the cleaning crew arriving today, first thing, and he wanted to be there when they arrived. Carol wouldn't be there, she had to feed her guests. But he wanted to be useful, so she didn't send him packing.

After she'd kicked him out last night, he'd gone to Greg's bar to talk to Greg and Terry who were both there. When he'd first walked in, he'd seen the two men exchange glances and they'd marched him into Greg's office, which was just fine with him.

Things had gotten a little heated to begin with, Greg and Terry in his face, over hurting Carol, and him right back in theirs, for starting it all. For stirring up trouble, by butting their noses in. It had taken them a while to air their grievances. Fortunately, none of them were hotheads so it had all been verbal.

When everyone had calmed down, they had a shot and then he'd asked them for help.

Terry had been aghast. "You want our help to convince

Mom to give you a second chance? Are you kidding me right now? Why in the hell do you think I would be interested in doing that?"

He didn't want to tell the men what he'd realized before he had a chance to tell Carol. That he loved her and wanted to spend the rest of his life with her. So instead he said, "I think your mother is an exceptional woman and I want to see where this might lead."

Terry started to speak but Greg held up a hand. "How committed to this are you?"

"Fully. I brought my workstation from the office and put my house on the market."

Terry's mouth dropped open, but Greg just nodded and poured them another shot. He lifted his glass. "To second chances."

After tossing the shot back Terry said, "So this is serious. What kind of help did you want?"

Max enjoyed the burn of the liquor and said quietly, "Just some ideas on how to... how to romance her. Amber suggested she'd not had much of that in her life, marriage to your father had been the two of them starting in grade school and never deviating from that path. She thought Carol might like to be wooed."

Terry nodded. "That's pretty much the way it happened. Dad was a good man, but I'm not sure he ever did much to demonstrate what she meant to him. At least not anything us kids could see."

Max said, "I thought about flowers, candy, and jewelry, but..."

Greg muttered, "Cliché."

"Exactly. I want to do something that's unique to Carol. I know she likes this library project and I plan to keep involved in that."

Terry nodded. "Acts of service, that's always good. She

told me she needed some help clearing the land around the Zimmerman place for more parking."

Greg frowned and shook his head. "Lining someone up to do that might be good, but that kind of work needs a backhoe, chainsaws, and shredders. Plus, stuff like that is nice and might get you some points, but it's not exactly romantic."

"Maybe take her out dancing, she does love music. Perhaps to Chelan for the night, we could get Sandy to help at the inn for a day or two." Terry said.

An idea was starting to form in his mind. Max knew she liked metal music and heavy rock. "Good to know, I could get her away for a day or two."

"Sure, Sandy knows it all, from when Mom had surgery."

Max had gone back to his hotel and made a list of everything he could think of. Even though flowers were a cliché, they were one because they *worked*. He'd gotten online and had a bouquet ordered to be delivered at nine this morning to the inn. She would still be busy with guests and breakfast, but that would be a good thing in this case. He hoped some tourist would gush over them.

After he'd ordered the flowers, he'd done a bit more research, pleased to find two different ways to surprise her with a day or two off from the B&B.

He stopped by the bakery for something for breakfast, he'd not ever stopped in before, since Carol had kept him well fed in the mornings. The bakery was filled with an assortment of heavenly treats.

The woman behind the counter looked at him through narrowed eyes. "You're back."

He looked behind him at the empty space and then turned back. "Um, excuse me, have we met?"

"Not exactly, but I saw you with Carol a few times." She crossed her arms over her chest and looked decidedly unfriendly.

Dammit, he didn't even know who this woman was, and she was giving him a hard time. Towns of this size and the way news travelled, were a mystery to him. "Yes. I came back. I realized I'd left something precious behind, and came back to see if I could have another chance."

The woman's expression eased a tiny bit, so he took advantage of that. "Can I get some coffee and some food?"

"Why aren't you eating at Carol's?"

"I'm staying in the hotel."

The woman laughed. "Good for Carol. Yes, I suppose I can get you some coffee and breakfast."

He pulled out his thermos. "Can I get a large cup and also this filled up? Is there anything Carol is particularly fond of? Or Patty Anne?"

She nodded. "So, you're working at the Zimmerman place with them, but staying at the hotel. Interesting."

"Since you are so enjoying my misery can you tell me your name?"

She pulled the apron down and pointed to the nametag. "Samantha. The pin likes to hide, but most people know me, so it doesn't matter."

"Kind of nice to meet you, Samantha."

She laughed and he felt like maybe he'd won her over just a smidgeon.

Carol was chatting up a family at breakfast, when the room grew quiet. She turned around and standing in the doorway was a huge bouquet of flowers, there were feet under them, so she knew someone was holding the enormous spray, but they were completely obscured by the arrangement.

She walked over. "Jeb, is that you behind those flowers?"

The flowers answered, "Yes Carol, it's me. Where do you want these?"

Carol looked around, she didn't really have space for something that size, but Jeb couldn't just stand there and hold them all day. There was a table that was off to the side not being used, so she decided it would have to do. "That table for two, to your right, will do for now."

Jeb walked slowly to the table and set his burden down with a little huff. The guy was in his nineties, most of the flower deliveries in the town were for tiny little arrangements. She reached in her pocket, glad she'd put some cash in there before she'd come down to make breakfast. She gave Jeb five dollars and he slowly moved back through the inn to the front door.

She pulled out the card, which read, "So sorry, can we be friends again? Max," she sighed and supposed they could be friends, but this arrangement was ridiculous, she would break it up and put fresh flowers in each room, including hers. The wall around her heart cracked a little and a piece fell out, she hadn't been given flowers by a man in many, many years.

After the guests had gone on their merry ways and she'd cleaned up the breakfast, Carol took the huge arrangement to the kitchen and pulled out all the vases she had. Both Judy and Karen exclaimed over the bouquet.

"It is gorgeous, but it's too big to keep in one place, so I want to divide it up. We'll put part of it in reception and part in the dining room. Then I want vases put in all the guest rooms while you clean them, Karen. You each can take some home with you too. I'll keep some for my room also." She looked at the flowers. "Perhaps I'll keep the roses."

Judy said, "Oh yes, you should keep the roses. Everyone else can have all the other flowers."

"That's very generous of you, Carol. You've got yourself an admirer," Karen replied.

"They're from Max and he's trying to get out of the doghouse for leaving so abruptly."

Karen laughed. "Men can be so stupid. But at least he's got good taste, I'll bet he cleared out Laura's whole shop with that purchase. She can probably take the day off."

Carol raised her eyebrows in surprise. "I hadn't thought about that. I hope Laura charged him a bundle."

Judy laughed. "I want to be just like you when I grow up, Carol."

Later, Carol packed herself a lunch to take to the Zimmerman's place, she might have added a little more to it, not for Max of course, but just in case someone was hungry, besides herself. She took a few extra drinks, also. She had one flower in her hair from the bouquet, to show Max she had accepted his gift.

Entering the parlor, she saw him hard at work. It looked like the cleaning crew had managed to get the room clean. The windows sparkled and the walls were cobweb free. The floors were clean, but she could see a few places where they needed to be refinished. She was glad they were hard wood, the rug in the center of the room had been vacuumed and looked so much brighter than she'd thought it would be. It was quite a lovely room, all cleaned up.

"Oh my, it's so clean and pretty, how long did it take them to clean this room?"

Max looked up and his eyes zeroed in on the flower. "About an hour. You got my flowers."

"I did, they are gorgeous, thank you."

"So, can we be friends again?"

"Yes, we can. I'm a little surprised Laura had enough flowers for that gigantic display."

He shuffled his feet. "When she called to confirm the order, she did say I was going to clear her out of flowers."

"You didn't need to go quite so overboard. I couldn't even see Jeb when he delivered it."

"No, I screwed up big, so the flowers had to be big too. I really am sorry I got so freaked out, and ran away in a panic."

"What made you so frightened?"

"My feelings for you. They were growing so fast, overwhelming me, I wasn't sure it was a good thing."

Carol could understand feeling overwhelmed, but not the running away part. It still hurt her feelings that he hadn't talked to her about it. She didn't know why he'd come back and wasn't ready to hear it. She wanted to enjoy her flower gift, and not look too closely at the why for it. "Well, I need to get busy. Thank you again for the flowers."

She fled the room leaving Max with an odd expression on his face.

When their agreed upon late lunch time rolled around, they decided to eat in the newly cleaned kitchen. It nearly made her eyes hurt it was so sparkling. She didn't know if the refrigerator or oven worked, but by golly they were spotless. She'd told the cleaning crew to dispose of any curtains or rugs or furnishings that were beyond repair, so the windows in the kitchen and breakfast nook were bare, and shining with the summer sun.

Max said, "Wow, we almost need sunglasses to eat in here." He walked over to the fridge that Carol noticed seemed to be humming away. Pulling it open Max said, "It's getting cold, looks like it still works." He opened the freezer door and nodded. "They don't make them like they used to. I don't know how long it will run, but it's working fine now. Even the freezer."

"That's great. I'll get if filled with some water and a few supplies, so we don't have to cart food every day."

They sat at the table in the breakfast nook and everyone piled the food on the table. There was enough food for three days as each one of them had packed more than they needed. The pièce de résistance was the bakery box Max put in the middle of the table. "I went by the bakery this morning and Samantha told me what you ladies fancied, so I bought some. And added a few brownies too."

When he opened the box, Carol gasped, and Patty Anne clapped her hands. "Yay, for you and Samantha."

Carol's favorite dark chocolate and Chantilly cream horns were right there, two of them. Another piece of the wall around her heart splintered and fell to the ground. But that wasn't the last one.

Every day after that Max did something sweet. A card left in the bookcase she was working on, a slice of pie from Amber's restaurant magically appearing in her refrigerator at the B&B, balloons tied to her car. A pair of earrings she'd admired at the art gallery, wrapped in gold paper with a bow, was on the kitchen counter, when she got up at three thirty in the morning. More flowers arrived about every four days, just about the time the others were starting to wilt, on and on it went, and every day another chunk of the wall fell.

She found out Max had rented a fully furnished vacation rental in town, one that had been leased for the summer, but the family had not been able to stay due to a grandmother's health. He could have it for as long as he wanted until next summer when it was booked again.

One night, after working all day in the Zimmerman house, Max asked her if he could take her out for dinner the following night to Amber's fancy side of the restaurant. Patty Anne had plans for that same night, so they'd decided to knock off early. Carol had been anticipating a long soak in the tub, and then an early night in her jammies, in front of the TV.

Max looked so earnest and pleading, that she gave in. They'd not spent any alone time, other than a few short moments, while she'd thanked him for his gifts. They'd still not talked anything through, and she supposed it was time. There wasn't much left of the wall around her heart, and he'd been working non-stop at the library, even starting on the trailers in the yard.

"Yes, Max, I will come to dinner with you."

His smile of joy did something funny to her insides and she hoped she wasn't making a huge mistake.

CHAPTER THIRTY-SIX

*M*ax was a basket case. Tonight, was his big push. He was going to lay all his cards out on the table, and hope like hell she didn't tell him he'd lost his chance. He'd wracked his brains thinking of everything he could to romance her. Tonight, was his last big hurrah. If he failed, however, he had every intention of continuing his campaign of romance. He'd just have to find new ways to do it. God help him.

He'd made reservations with Amber and asked for a secluded table. It might be presumptuous of him, but he'd pre-ordered the meal also. He knew her tastes well enough, and it would limit interaction with the staff, he didn't want anyone to interrupt, once he had her all to himself.

Max slipped his last gift into the upper pocket of his suit coat and walked out of the vacation rental. It was still too warm out for a suit, but he'd made early dinner reservations, Carol got up at three in the morning, so it needed to be an early meal.

He'd thought about getting her a corsage, but then decided he was being foolish, this wasn't prom. She had a houseful of flowers that had been delivered just this morn-ing. He might just keep that flower delivery as a standing order regardless of what happened tonight. The woman deserved them, and he was now Laura's best customer, she'd said something about surpassing Chris.

Max drove to the B&B and parked in front rather than in the rear parking area. He debated whether he should walk in or ring the doorbell. As a guest he'd always walked in and everyone else seemed to do that, but he wanted this to be special. Still, her having to hurry to the door of her business was not the tone he wanted to set either. He opted to walk in the door and wait for her to come down.

He propped himself against the wall at the foot of the stairs, Carol was always prompt, so he knew it wouldn't be a long wait. When she started down the stairs, he was glad he was propped up by the wall, because she looked magnificent and so damn sexy, he wasn't sure his knees would keep him upright.

She had on a knee length black dress that clung exactly where it should and flared at the bottom, the top was all lacy and sleeveless. Over the dress she wore a see-through white jacket that skimmed her hips and had more lace on the sleeves and hem. There were strappy black sandals on her feet, and he wanted to kiss the toes peeking out of them. She wore the earrings he'd picked out for her, and carried a small clutch.

He wasn't sure he could think, let alone speak, she was killing him.

She got to the bottom of the stairs and raised one eyebrow. "Well?"

He shook his head like he was coming out of a daze, which he was, and walked forward. He took her hand and raised it to his lips. Watching her face, he softly kissed her fingers. Max saw her melt just a little, while fire rushed through his veins.

"You look amazing. I was trapped in a haze of admiration, watching you come down the stairs."

She laughed. "You are looking pretty hot yourself."

"I can clean up when I need to. Are you ready?"

She nodded, so he threaded her hand through his arm, and they walked into the warm summer night.

Carol was glad she'd decided to go out with Max. It was time to find out what he was up to, with all the gifts. The first few had been apology gifts, but they had continued. Every single day there was something. Even if it was just a note remembering something they had shared. Was he trying to get back to their former closeness? He hadn't made any sort of move, just friendly chatting and small tokens. The uncertainty was driving her crazy.

Yes, it was time to get it all out on the table. Come what may.

Max was being the consummate gentleman, opening doors, holding her chair, pouring them wine, from the bottle in the ice bucket by their table. They'd only been seated a moment when the waitress set salads in front of them, asking if they wanted fresh cheese grated on top, or pepper, then whisking away.

"I ordered for both of us, so we don't have the waitress hovering. I wanted you all to myself."

That was kind of odd, but he looked so endearing that she didn't mind. Nothing Amber served was bad and he might have paid attention enough earlier this summer that he could know her preferences.

She took a sip of wine and gave him the go-ahead look.

He picked up his fork with salad on it and then set it back on his plate. She ate a small bite to keep herself from grinning at his nervousness.

He cleared his throat and took a gulp of wine. "The day I left, Greg... No, I can't blame it on Greg, all he did was get me thinking. I'd never planned to stay, you knew that, and I knew that, but something he said made me picture it, and it hurt. Thinking about actually leaving hurt, I didn't want to leave you."

That didn't make any sense. He didn't want to leave, but he had immediately. She gave him a confused frown.

"I know what you're thinking, then why did I run out of town like my pants were on fire?"

"Something like that."

"Because I was afraid of falling more in love with you than I already had, because leaving then would be even harder. So, I bailed, terrified to stay even one more minute in your presence."

Okay that made sense in a kind of twisted way, but... "Then why are you back?"

"Because, my brother, told me I was a dumbass for leaving."

Carol listened to all Max had to say about how he'd been living before coming to Chedwick, and then about the discoveries he had made, as he'd wandered through his house. But none of that answered her real question. "So, you love Chedwick enough to uproot your life and move here?"

"No, silly, I love you, enough to uproot my life and move. I came with only one purpose, and that was to convince you to spend your life with me."

He reached into his jacket pocket and her heart stopped. Was he asking her to marry him? They didn't really know each other well enough. But he didn't put a ring on the table. He put an envelope down and pushed it toward her.

Curious, she picked it up and lifted the flap, inside were tickets, like for a sporting event. Curiouser and curiouser. She pulled out her reading glasses, because it was dim in their secluded corner. There were four tickets, two each for two different venues. One was for the Rolling Stones in Seattle in the fall, and the other was for Aerosmith, in Las Vegas, at the start of the new year.

Her eyes filled up with tears and her throat closed. Max did know her, he'd picked the perfect gift to show her. She pulled off her glasses and wiped her eyes, probably ruining her mascara, but she didn't care, she could fix it later. She might have used the waterproof one to begin with.

Carol looked up to see Max looking apprehensive. She smiled a smile that started at her toes and filled her whole body, shining out of her eyes and lifting her lips. "All right Max, I will spend my life with you."

His whole being relaxed, and a smile came over his features, also. "Thank God. I was running out of ideas. Not that I intend to stop romancing you, ever, but maybe I can do it more up close and personal."

She lifted her glass of wine. "To up close and personal."

The waitress came out with their entrees and rolled her eyes at their untouched salads. They moved their salads to the side. They could enjoy them with their entrees. Carol looked down at her plate, and it was exactly what she would have ordered. Yep, the man knew her pretty darn well.

EPILOGUE

ax and Carol stood side by side, both of their hands on the handle, ready to cut as soon as the photographer gave them the nod. They'd asked Deborah to do the honors, she'd been back every few months, for over a year, taking pictures of Chedwick in every season for the coffee table book her publisher had commissioned her to do. Both Carol and Max liked her work, so they invited her to be a part of their big day.

Deborah got it framed just right and gave them the nod, they smiled at each other and cut the ribbon, as a cheer rose up. The Zimmerman Public Library was officially open, and Mr. and Mrs. Max Radcliff couldn't be happier.

Max and Carol stood to the side hand in hand as the whole town rushed in to see the new town library, especially the secret tower in the middle.

Janet and her two kids came up, Janet giving both Carol and Max a hug. "Mom, this is a great thing you've done. You too, Max. The kids are so excited."

Gerald who had just turned twelve said, "I hope there are some Tamora Pierce books in here."

Carol put her hand on his shoulder, he was 'too old' for hugs. "I think I saw some."

Carrie who was eight and not reading very well yet said, "I'm hoping for some silly joke books. I love to tell jokes."

Carol hugged her granddaughter. Of course, she'd made sure the library had the kinds of books her grandchildren wanted to read. "There just might be."

Janet ushered her children in the door. She was looking so much better, now that her ex-husband was behind bars and unable to hurt her anymore. It had almost killed Carol, to sit by and watch her beautiful daughter die slowly, at the hands of that cruel bastard.

They'd all tried to convince her to leave him, but she never said a word, blaming the bruises on falling, or other nonsense. Until the day he'd pushed Gerald hard enough to break his arm. That had been the end of Janet's silence.

Greg and Sandy came up next, Carol suspected Sandy might be pregnant, but she and Greg had not mentioned it, so neither did Carol.

"Mom, this is so exciting. You and Max did a terrific job."

Max said, "We're very happy with the way it turned out."

Carol nodded. "And I think the Zimmermans would be pleased."

"I know they would, the Anderson-Zimmerman connection is alive and well." Greg said. Sandy put her hand through Greg's arm, and they walked into the library.

Carol had laughed when she'd gotten to the part of the book that explained the Anderson and Zimmerman connection. The two families had engaged in some stupid feud for twenty years about an apple tree that grew on the border between their lands. Then a Zimmerman boy had fallen in love with an Anderson girl and the couple had convinced the two families to deed them the land the apple tree grew on, to build their house.

They'd started with a small log cabin and had eventually built the large mansion that now housed the library. The apple tree was at the back of the kitchen garden, one of the ones Max had pointed out on their first day, the others in the orchard had come from seeds planted from that old, gnarled tree.

So now the library stood on Anderson land with the Zimmerman name on the front. Quite a fitting ending to the story, in her opinion.

Terry interrupted her musings with a hug and then he shook Max's hand. "I'm still not happy about you two eloping, but you did a damn fine job on the library."

Deborah who was taking pictures of the hordes entering the library said, "It's their life Terry Anderson, not yours."

"She's my mother."

"So what? That gives you the right to dictate her life?" Deborah started to follow the crowd and Terry marched right along arguing with her, without a goodbye or glance back to Carol and Max.

Carol looked at Max and grinned. "I'm so glad she said that. Leaves us free to enjoy the day. He can go bicker with her."

Max watched them go. "It's kind of out of character for Terry, he's usually pretty laid back and mellow."

"Not when she's around. I don't know why she rubs him wrong, but she does. Well that, and us getting married in Las Vegas after the Aerosmith concert."

Max rubbed his neck. "Yeah, he's been kind of a pain about that."

"He's the baby, he'll have to get over it. I thought the timing was perfect."

Carol and Max were alone on the porch, so he kissed her long and slow. "I thought it was perfect timing too. Just the two of us, no muss, no fuss."

Carol pulled him back for another kiss, they'd both had large first weddings, that had been beautiful and stressful. Theirs had been sweet and special, in a little bridal place, that set just the right note, for another chance for love.

The End

If you enjoyed this story, please consider leaving a review at your favorite retailer, Bookbub, or Goodreads.
Thanks!

BURLAP AND BARBED WIRE SERIES

Colorado Cowboys

A Cowboy for Alyssa: Burlap and Barbed Wire #1

Beau and Alyssa's story

Taming Adam: Burlap and Barbed Wire #2

Adam and Rachel's story

Tempting Chase: Burlap and Barbed Wire #3

Chase and Katie's story

Roping Cade: Burlap and Barbed Wire #4

Cade and Summer's story

Trusting Drew: Burlap and Barbed Wire #5

Drew and Lily's story

Emma's Rodeo Cowboy: Burlap and Barbed Wire #6

Emma and Zach's story

SADDLES AND SECRETS SERIES

Wyoming Wranglers

The Lawman: Saddles and Secrets #1

Maggie Ann and John's story

The Watcher: Saddles and Secrets #2

Christina and Rob's story

The Rescuer: Saddles and Secrets #3

Milly and Tim's story

The Vacation: Saddles and Secrets Short Story

Andrea and Carl Ray's story

(Part of the Getting Wild in Deadwood anthology)

STAND ALONE

Helluva Engineer

Patricia and Steve's story

ABOUT THE AUTHOR

What does a geeky math nerd know about writing romance?

That's a darn good question. As a former techy I've done everything from computer programming to international trainer. Prior to college I had lots of different jobs and activities that were so diverse, I was an anomaly.

None of that qualifies me for writing novels. But I have some darn good stories to tell and a lot of imagination.

I have lived in Colorado, Hawaii and currently reside in Washington. Going from two states with 340 days of sun to a state with 340 days of clouds, I had to do something to perk me up. And that's when I started this new adventure called author. Joining the Romance Writers of America and two local chapters, helped me learn the craft quickly and has been a ton of fun.

My family consists of two grown children, their spouses, two adorable grand-daughters, and one grand dog. My favorite activity is playing with my granddaughters!

When the girls can't play with their amazing grandmother, my interests are reading and writing, yay! I started reading at a young age with the Nancy Drew mysteries and have continued to be an avid reader my whole life. My favorite reading material is romance, but occasionally if other stories creep into my to-be-read pile, I don't kick them out.

Some of the strange jobs I have held are a carnation grower's worker, a trap club puller, a pizza hut waitress, a software engineer, an international trainer, and a business program manager. I took welding, drafting and upholstery in high school, a long time ago, when girls didn't take those classes, so I have an eclectic bunch of knowledge and experience.

And for something really unusual... I once had a raccoon as a pet.

Join with me as I tell my stories, weaving real tidbits from my life in with imaginary ones. You'll have to guess which is which. It will be a hoot!

Contact me: www.shirleypenick.com

To sign up for Shirley's Monthly Newsletter, sign up on my website or send email to shirleypenick@outlook.com, subject newsletter.

Follow me:

facebook.com/ShirleyPenickAuthorFans
twitter.com/shirley_penick
instagram.com/shirleypenickauthor
bookbub.com/authors/shirley-penick
goodreads.com/shirleypenick